While Caroline was talking about cooking, her eyes had glistened with enthusiasm. Her speech had become light and quick with excitement. Her smile had been easy and often. But most of all, her comfortable laughter had rung with a freedom which created something similar to magic. Assistant District Attorney VanDere was no longer average in her appearance, she was stunning.

Caroline began to blush when she handed Tenny a glass of wine and noticed her admiration. She turned back to the stove. "So I'm actually kind of a fan of yours."

"Oh really?" Tenny found it hard to believe after the berating she had received.

"Yeah. I saw the television special about your rape investigation. I was very touched by it." Caroline faced her again.

"Then you're a fan of Diane Barker. It was her program." Compliments made Tenny uncomfortable.

Caroline was direct. "No, I think you were the key to the whole investigation. You held your team together. You got the community together. Besides, you're the one that finally caught that bastard."

It was Tenny's turn to look away. "Well, I wish you would give me that much credit now."

The comment made Caroline pause. "I guess I did come off a little hard earlier." Caroline appeared to be at a loss for words. "It's just . . . it means so much to me to stop them."

Tenny was looking Caroline in the eyes. "Not nearly as much as it means to me."

About the Author

Melanie McAllester spent over ten years as a police officer for the Palo Alto Police Department in the San Francisco Bay Area. She specialized in crisis resolution intervention and hazardous materials response. She also has a Bachelor's degree in Political Science and a Master's degree in Public Administration. Recently she and her partner relocated to the Seattle area where she will continue her career in the public sector. Her first book, *The Lessons* (published by Spinsters Ink, 1994), introduced her feature character Elizabeth (Tenacity) Mendoza and brought together Tenny's team.

THE
SEARCH

by
Melanie McAllester

THE NAIAD PRESS, INC.
1996

Printed in the United States of America on acid-free paper
First Edition

Editor: Christine Cassidy
Cover designer: Bonnie Liss (Phoenix Graphics)
Typesetter: Sandi Stancil

Library of Congress Cataloging-in-Publication Data

McAllester, Melanie. 1962–
    The search / by Melanie McAllester.
        p.   cm.
    ISBN 1-56280-150-3 (pbk.)
    I. Title.
PS3563.C266S43   1996
813'.54—dc20
                                                95-44437
                                                CIP

Acknowledgments

I would like to thank Agent Carole Baldwin of the Palo Alto Police for planting the seed in my head which became a novel and for sharing her knowledge of child abductions with me. Thanks also to Jean Krahulec for her excellent language skills. Finally, a special thanks to Lisa Talbott for introducing me to parenthood, even for a short period. It allowed me to write this novel with feeling and not just words.

BOOK ONE

Chapter One

It wasn't pain anymore. It was an incredible fire in her legs. Her muscles twinged and shook, placing her on the edge of control, but still she continued cranking. Pulling harder with her arms, she tried to relieve some of the fatigue in her legs. Yet the intense heat, the burning, the weariness just moved to her arms. Then it slowly spread to her shoulders and moved down her back. Muscles she didn't know she had were tightening, straining and complaining. Her body was about to quit, but her mind was focused ahead, refusing to acknowledge her body's desperate warnings of near total exhaustion.

"Damn her! I can't believe I let her talk me into this. What was I thinking? Me on a damn bike. I must be crazy. I'm going to kill her." Tenny's breathless argument with nobody kept her from feeling the heat. She let her anger fuel the fire and kept pedaling.

The young man who had just snatched the purse was only about thirty yards ahead of her and climbing one of the many steep hills of Bayview. This was not his first crime. In fact he was wanted by officers all over the city. He had committed violent, bold crimes. It didn't seem to make a difference to him who the victim was, how much he got or how many people witnessed his attacks. He struck at whim and always eluded capture, never making mistakes. But on this September afternoon he had made one — he had committed his crime on Tenny's beat.

The suspect made a right turn and was momentarily out of Tenny's view. If he was smart, he would bail off his bicycle and attempt to hide from Tenny. It should be obvious to him, she thought, that she was not going to give up and that his endurance was matched by her desire to apprehend him. Tenny hoped he was as logical as she was as she rounded the corner.

"Damn, this guy is out of his mind. He must be high." Tenny swore as she spotted him standing on his pedals and pumping his bicycle up a steeper hill. She wanted to jump off her bicycle and run up and grab this punk. Yet her instincts warned her that the moment she dismounted her legs would fail. She needed to radio her location to the officers responding in cars, but if she let go of the handlebars to key her mike, she was sure to crash. The whole locomotion up the hill depended on a delicate balance of movement over two wheels. She wanted to stop, but if she did then he would win. Nobody beat Tenny. Her job was more than a game.

Over the radio, Tenny could hear her fellow officers anxiously requesting her present location. A siren wailed as police vehicles maneuvered through the noontime traffic. Help was close. It was just a matter of moments before

4

one of her partners would stumble into her pursuit. *Push, pull. Push, pull. Keep going. Keep going. Can't stop. Don't stop!* Tenny silently chanted.

Closing in on him, she neared the top of the hill. Still, her partners hadn't found Tenny and she knew that if the suspect made it to the top of the hill, he'd be gone. He'd already eluded them many times before on that bicycle. He was fearless, darting in and out of traffic in a kamikaze manner which paralyzed pursuing police cars. Tenny needed help and she needed it fast.

An engine roared behind her and a siren blasted a modern-day bugle charge. Tenny glanced over her shoulder and spotted help two blocks back at the bottom of the hill. The suspect was only a few yards from the top. She pushed harder, her legs numb. The police vehicle growled as the officer down-shifted. They had to overtake the suspect before he crested the hill.

"No, no, no — stop! Stop!" Tenny's commands were emitted and immediately sucked back in as she gulped for air. He'd made it over the top, gone from view once again. When she crested the hill, she saw the suspect coasting wildly, confident of his escape. Tenny started to coast in pursuit, the police unit behind her still a block away. She heard the officer alert the other units in the area that the suspect was on a downhill course.

His speed was incredible. He was evidently fearless, not using his brakes as he careened down the hill. Tenny watched a marked unit pull in front of him as he approached the first intersection. Without any hesitation the suspect jumped the curb between two parked cars and used the sidewalk to evade the roadblock. Just like he had done before.

Tenny thrust her bicycle into the highest gear and instead of coasting, she began to pedal. If he got away it would be only hours before he struck again. Over the last few weeks he was becoming progressively violent during his attacks. What if the next time he seriously injured somebody or even killed? Tenny couldn't let that happen. He might be fearless, but she was tenacious.

He glanced over his shoulder and seemed surprised to find the cop-on-a-bike barreling down upon him. Traveling at speeds unsafe for cars, they propelled themselves through the deadly traffic. Tenny saw everything but comprehended nothing. Her brain didn't have enough time to record what her body's response would be before the next movement came. Turning, skidding, pedaling, riding against traffic, riding through traffic — a race to the end, whatever it might be.

Tenny was only about twenty-five feet behind him as they neared a busy intersection. He began to brake as he checked for a safe passage through the fast-moving traffic. Tenny pedaled harder. It was her chance. That's when it happened. Everything went so fast, Tenny only had time for "Oh shit!" Two famous words among the police community. When uttered it meant that the officer had stepped beyond planning and control. Her only hope was instinct, training and luck.

The car rolled into the intersection and the driver casually glanced to his right. When he saw the two bicyclists speeding in his direction, his natural reaction brought the car to a jolting halt right in their path. The suspect was able to brake and bring his rear tire around in a controlled skid. He lay his bicycle down, sliding into and partially under the car. Tenny was not as fortunate.

The instant she realized that she was going to crash she attempted to brake. In fear she clamped down on both brakes simultaneously, bringing the bicycle to a sudden standstill and launching her through the handlebars. Sailing over the car's hood, she tried to kick free of the toe clips but couldn't. Her trusty bicycle followed as she flew through the air. She was easily three feet above the hood, bicycle dangling dangerously from her feet, dragging across the hood with a horrifying screech of metal on metal.

Tenny freed herself somehow from the binding toe clips, but her foot was instantly ensnared between the bicycle's front tire and the frame. The front tire spun once and her bicycle transformed into a vise as it pressed on Tenny's ankle. In a horrifying instant of clarity, Tenny imagined the impact with the ground would sever her foot from the rest of her body.

Tenny didn't remember hitting the ground. Legs and bicycle hopelessly soaring above her, Tenny's right shoulder absorbed the initial collision, immediately dislocating. Pain shot through her as her head slammed to the pavement. The concussion didn't knock her unconscious, but it did divert her mind from the pain which the rest of her body was enduring.

Next to land was her right hip, which hosted her 9mm, semi-automatic handgun. The bulletproof vest was the only thing preventing the gun from cracking several of her ribs. The contusion the gun delivered to her unprotected hip would leave a permanent bruise. Finally Tenny's legs slammed to the ground, bringing the bike down on top of her.

A woman leaped from the car and rushed to Tenny's side. Tenny was already struggling to free herself from the bicycle, concerned only about the suspect's escape.

"Don't move! Please don't move, you're hurt." The woman was gently restraining Tenny and trying to calm her.

Two police vehicles screeched to a stop and two officers

vaulted toward the suspect. With his broken leg, it was clear he wasn't about to go anywhere. The other two rushed at the woman, uncomfortable with anybody being that close to one of their own.

"Officer down! We need medics, code three." The younger female officer was speaking frantically into her radio.

The male officer pushed the woman away from Tenny. Pushing harder than he should have. Tenny thought his own adrenaline and concern for her was releasing itself on this stranger.

"I'm a doctor. Let me help." The woman moved back toward her. This time the male officer gently grabbed the doctor's arm and brought her in close again. "Just try to keep her still. I think she's going into shock."

"I'm not going into shock! Just get this fucking thing off me."

"Tenny, just do what the doctor says. Medics are on the way and that shithead is cuffed. Just relax!" Bud Norman, who had been one of Tenny's training officers, said as he tried to free Tenny's legs from the bicycle's grip.

"Shit! Not that way, Bud." Tenny winced as the vise tightened on her ankle.

The female officer stepped in. "Here, let me." She held the bike up as Bud carefully twisted the front tire in the opposite direction, freeing Tenny.

Blood gushed from the deep cuts and the doctor reached for the injured ankle.

Tenny tried to stand. "I'm fine, you guys. Just help me up."

Finally the doctor had enough of Tenny's foolish heroics. "Look, I'm the doctor not you. You're injured, so sit still!"

Nobody snapped at her like that except maybe her mother. Startled, Tenny looked at the woman for the first

8

time. She had one brown eye and one blue eye. It was incredible, and a little inhuman. The pain took advantage of the momentary lapse in concentration and swept into her head. Suddenly every inch of her hurt. More sirens were approaching and she saw the medic van sway around the corner. She lay back as the doctor reassured her. Tenny was ready to call it a day.

"She's asleep," Ashley whispered from the doorway of the hospital room.

"What're you whispering for? She's in there and we're out here." Steve started to push by Ashley. "Let's wake her up. She's probably only sleeping because she's bored."

Ashley grabbed his arm. "We're not going in."

Ashley squeezed his arm tighter. She was muscular and strong, but she knew that this spontaneous tug-of-war was no contest.

Steve smiled. "Sure we are," and he dragged Ashley easily into the room.

"You shithead. You always have to have everything your way."

Steve seemed to ignore her as he released himself and walked up to the bed. Ashley could tell that the sight of Tenny's battered body brought back memories as his mood instantly mellowed.

"Tenny, you sleeping?"

Ashley jabbed him. "I told you she was."

Tenny's eyes sprang open and the smile that her friends had grown accustomed to greeted them. "How could anybody sleep with all the noise you two make."

"I tried to tell him, but he just had to do things his way."

"Actually I was just bored. There's nothing to do but sleep in this place."

9

Steve turned triumphantly to Ashley but didn't say anything.

The three of them had been friends for almost a year. They had been selected from different jurisdictions for a joint investigation to hunt a serial rapist who was attacking only lesbians. Tenny had been a homicide detective for Bayview and was chosen for her tenacious investigative style. Ashley had been a rookie cop with an impressive record of felony arrests during her two years with the Los Palos Police in Southern California. Both were also selected by their respective departments because of their sexual orientation, and they understood their extraordinary duty in the investigation and were determined to stop the rapist. This had not been the case for Steve.

He had earned his position on the team by default — he was Los Palos' sexual assault detective. At first the only thing Steve contributed to the team was his dislike for homosexuals and his intolerance for his partners. Tenny and Ashley had found themselves battling two men full of prejudice, each dangerous in his own way.

Yet as the team's pursuit of the rapist continued, Steve discovered that his hate had been manufactured by myths. He allowed himself to learn from his experiences during their investigation. Afterward, they found themselves forever bound to one another. They had become special friends. Now any excuse was enough for them to travel up and down California to visit. There was no way Steve and Ashley would not have been beside Tenny while she was hospitalized.

Steve sat in the chair next to the bed as Ashley watched from the doorway. "You're all right, aren't you?"

Tenny's right arm was wrapped to her chest because of her shoulder separation, but she reached awkwardly across her body with her left hand until Steve caught it and it disappeared in his own huge hand.

"I'm fine."

"Your mom called us," Steve reassured her. "We came right away."

"What about work?"

Steve laughed. "Come on, you know what it's like out of patrol. Things are flexible."

Ashley watched as Tenny touched Steve's face. It was her best way of thanking them. Her own hands were shoved deep into her jeans pockets. Shuffling slightly in place, Ashley wanted out of this room — too many memories. Hospitals made Ashley feel helpless. It had been a room like this one that she had been forced into by the rapist as he had finally vented his hate.

Tenny must have sensed Ashley's discomfort. "Tell you what. Why don't you guys bust me outta this place and I can tell you all about it over a beer."

Ashley liked this suggestion, and began to gather Tenny's stuff.

Steve didn't have to be convinced either. "Can you walk or do I need to get a wheelchair?"

"I can walk. I didn't break anything. I just have stitches in my ankle and bruises from head to toe."

Ashley came over and touched Tenny's cheekbone. "What about here?"

A large bandage covered most of her cheek. "A few more stitches. No big deal though, the doctor said the scar will barely be visible. Who knows, maybe it will make me look tougher. Like all those cops in the movies."

Tough was not a word Ashley would have used to describe Tenny, but she certainly didn't need a scar to add to her presence. Tenny was intimidating — not that she was physically threatening or mentally coercing. Instead it was her stunning features and mystical eyes which could create a daunting stare that few could endure. When she was angry or shy they called her the "ice woman" and she did nothing to change anyone's impression.

11

When she was in Homicide, her colleagues nicknamed her Tenacity. She would take a case and never let go, analyzing, interviewing, investigating and searching. She would sit for hours at a computer, spend days going over old cases and walk the streets looking for unidentified witnesses. Anything it took to solve a case. Her given name was Elizabeth, but Tenacity seemed to fit her better and even her family called her Tenny now.

Steve was reading her chart as she finished dressing. "You're scheduled for your tetanus booster at six." He glanced at his watch. "Shit, six-oh-two! Let's get outta here, ladies."

Ashley hesitated as they headed toward the door. "No, we'll get caught for sure. The nurse must be out there in the hall somewhere."

"It'll be no problem. We've done it before," Steve insisted.

"That was different. We had to then."

"Come on, Ashley, it's no big deal," Tenny said. "Nobody's gonna catch us."

They all stopped at the door as if they were making the great escape from a prison instead of just leaving a hospital where nobody could make you stay anyway.

Steve was the mastermind. "Okay, Ashley, you go first and Tenny, you go right behind her. I'll go last, nobody can see around me. Now Ashley, make sure you turn away from the desk when you hit the hall."

Tenny was ready and gently pushing on Ashley's back. "Yeah, that'll work, go on, Ashley. Hurry before it's too late."

Her heart racing, Ashley opened the door and casually stepped out into the hall. Looking somewhat disoriented, which often happened to visitors, she glanced down the hall in both directions. A group of nurses stood perilously close at the next room and blocked that escape. The other direction was clear but required them to pass directly in front of the nurses' station where a single sentry was seated. Ashley slowly started in that direction as the gentle shoving against her back grew agitated.

She walked stiffly down the hallway, as if Tenny had her at gunpoint. As they passed the nurses' station Tenny and then Steve paused to say a friendly hello to the nurse at the desk. Ashley hated their boldness and admired it at the same time. The three of them continued to stroll down the anonymous halls of the hospital. Three more victims caught within its maze.

Once outside Tenny burst out laughing. "Girl, you would think that we just robbed a bank from the way you look."

Ashley was chagrined. "Hey, I don't want to get in trouble, that's all."

Steve walked past them toward the car. "They don't care if she's there or not. It's only another free bed to them."

"Yeah, and besides, trouble's going to find us — it always does." Tenny started after Steve.

Chapter Two

Tall, slim and graceful, she was a beautiful child almost seven years old. Everybody kept trying to get her mother to sign her up for ballet. She looked like she belonged on her tiptoes, prancing effortlessly across a stage. Her mother and father were often mistaken for brother and sister, and their child shared their brunette hair and dark eyes. Yet the child insisted that her hair was more red than brown, and being the persuasive child that she was, others were convinced to notice the shimmering red highlights.

Of course her real beauty was not in her appearance but in her freedom of spirit, the concinnity that all children have before they learn to think and doubt too much.

Propped against the front door, Kelsey waited impatiently for her mother. The sun was creeping up the driveway so slowly that its advance was concealed to the human eye. She was determined, however, to capture its movement this morning and stared intently at the light waiting for it to invade another inch of the cool shade. Maybe if she was standing right at the border between today and last night she would be able to sight the light's convergence.

"Mom, hurry or I'm gonna be late for school. I'm waiting outside, okay?"

Before receiving a response, she yanked open the door and ran to the edge of the shade. Positioning her toes on the line, she folded her arms across her chest and waited, as if her stubborn stance would halt the sun.

For a moment she thought the sun had been intimidated by her presence and ceased its assault on the shade. Then slowly it ventured forward and hesitantly began to move over her feet and up her legs. Before she could retreat the sun had captured her in its radiance and brought a smile to her face. She may not have really seen its encroachment, but she would never forget the feeling of the sun spreading over, across and through her.

Kelsey had been so intent on challenging nature that she hadn't noticed the small blue car parked on the wrong side of the street a couple of houses away. She didn't even hear it when the man inside started the engine. In fact, she didn't even notice the car creeping toward her until it was almost directly in front of her. It came to a stop with the engine running and the man stepped out.

"Hi there. I hope you can help me. I lost my puppy and I think I saw him a second ago hiding right there." He pointed at a bush near where she stood.

She had been warned over and over about strangers, and as he came around the front of his car, she retreated a few steps. But he sounded friendly and didn't look like a bad person. He had on a nice white shirt and tie and wasn't weird-looking like all the bad guys on television. Plus he had lost his puppy. She wished she had a puppy.

He looked up and down along the street, but she knew he was just worried about his puppy. Then he walked up to the bush and started to peer around. "I hope my eyes weren't playing tricks on me. He's the cutest little puppy I've ever seen. I'd be really sad if I lost him."

Kelsey felt sad just thinking about ever losing a puppy. He was so lucky. She really wanted one, but Mom said she would have to wait until she was older.

Suddenly the man smiled. "Oh great, here he is. Thank goodness." He leaned down and started to reach into the bush. She crept up to his side hoping to see the puppy. Maybe he would let her pet it for a minute.

Before Kelsey could see the puppy, the man suddenly grabbed her and pulled her against him. Instantly he lifted her from the ground and covered her mouth with his hand. She hadn't thought to scream until it was too late. He was strong and he was hurting her as he ran back to the car. She wasn't frightened. She didn't really understand what was happening.

The man rushed around to the driver's door, threw her across the seat and jumped in behind the wheel. Speeding away from the house, she realized there was no puppy, her mom wasn't there, she wasn't even sure if her mom knew this man. Suddenly she was frightened. Nothing that had just happened made any sense, but she knew that this wasn't right. Her mom didn't know where she was. This was a bad thing. This was wrong. It was very bad. She began to cry.

"It was incredible. I mean, I felt so sharp, like nothing could stop me."

Steve tapped Tenny's sling. "Well, something stopped you."

They were in Tenny's kitchen the next morning and had been listening to her relive her bicycle chase again. It was a big deal, since Tenny had never been very athletic. It wasn't that she was uncoordinated, she was simply lazy. She didn't have to work out to look fit, so why bother?

It had been Ashley who convinced her to put in for Bayview's new bicycle patrol unit. Then it took Tenny almost six months to get into the type of shape she expected from herself. Of course, now she was the best rider on the unit and her number of arrests reflected it. But yesterday she had surprised even herself.

"I can't believe you made it up that hill." Ashley was teasing her. Tenny had shown them the route of her pursuit on the way home from the hospital.

Ashley actually had been impressed.

"Hey, when I heal, I'll beat your butt up it," Tenny challenged.

Steve laughed. "You really must have hit your head hard." Everybody knew that Ashley was the only true athlete at the table.

The telephone prevented Tenny's response as she jumped up to get it, forgetting her injured ankle. The pain left her breathless as she answered.

"Hi, I was just calling to see if you were okay." The

17

low deep voice made Tenny's heart beat fast for a moment. "I heard about your accident from a friend at the station." Diane seemed unsure of herself.

"I was going to call you." Tenny didn't really sound convincing, even to herself.

"Are Ashley and Steve there?"

"Yeah."

"Well, you're in good hands, as always." There was a long pause. "You take care."

"I will. Thanks for calling." Nothing else left to say, Tenny thought.

"Sure."

The weight of the phone seemed to quadruple as Tenny turned it off and her hand dropped to her side. She still did not know if she had done the right thing by letting Diane slip out of her life. Tenny had tried to love her, but something, or somebody, still stood in her way.

They had met during the rape investigation, when Diane's search for a powerful story brought her into Tenny's life. Diane said that what they felt was love, but Tenny wasn't so sure. Their infrequent dates had never resulted in anything more than an awkward friendship. Finally Diane had given up, accepting a job in New York which provided the opportunity to do the investigative reporting which she loved. It had also put the entire country between them.

Ashley was curious. "Diane?"

"Yeah, she heard about the accident."

Neither Steve or Ashley probed further. Tenny didn't like to discuss this area of her life. She wearily set the phone on the counter, but it instantly began to ring again. Hesitating, Tenny looked to Ashley and then to Steve, as if one of them might answer the call. Finally, she picked up the phone.

There was a sobbing, choking, hysterical voice on the other end which at first Tenny didn't recognize.

"Elizabeth, oh God, help us. I don't know what happened. Please help!"

Tenny froze as she distinguished the frightened and desperate voice asking for help. It was Carter, the woman she loved. "Carter? Carter, calm down. I don't understand. Calm down and tell me what you're talking about." She turned away from Steve and Ashley.

"Tenny, they got her. I was only a few minutes behind her, but they got her. She's gone, Tenny." Carter was almost screaming. "God, they took my baby!"

The panic was contagious. Tenny collapsed against the wall and listened.

So much information was colliding in Tenny's head, she barely heard what Carter was telling her. She was thinking of the last time she saw Carter. It had been a year ago when they still spent time together and Tenny got to see Kelsey. Yet the visits always seemed to end with Tenny or Carter feeling hurt again, unable to understand why they couldn't be together. Eventually it became too much and they decided to part permanently. Tenny would never forget the look in her eyes. Carter seemed to be pleading for Tenny to stay and at the same time pushing her away. Tenny had been so confused that all she could do was give up, not knowing where to begin in order to start over.

Finally Tenny said, "Where are you?"

"I'm at Carlmont P.D. with Detective Reese."

"I'll be right there." When Tenny set down the telephone, the trance was broken. She was in control, except for a hint of anger. She narrowed her eyes and clamped her jaw tight, then turned and went upstairs without saying a word.

Steve and Ashley boldly followed. "What is it, Tenny?"

They got no response as they watched her strap on her firearm and clip her badge onto her belt. It was almost as if they weren't there, her mind already planning, preparing to govern her heart's emotions so that they couldn't interfere. She grabbed a coat to cover the weapon and then paused for a moment as she looked at the painting over her bed.

The children were playing happily in a field full of colorful flowers. No toys, no jungle gym, no adults. Only children with their smiles and their imaginations. Free to laugh, free to trust, free to like and free to love. In the picture they were always safe. A tear finally broke and she quickly wiped it away.

She turned to her friends who stood patiently in the doorway, waiting for her to explain. "They took Kelsey."

Nothing more needed to be said. Steve scooped the car keys from on top of the dresser. "Come on, I'll drive."

Carter was exhausted from crying and answering all the questions. She had lost confidence in the detective assigned to find her baby. He was focused on the assumption that her ex-husband had abducted Kelsey. Carter sat quietly in her chair. There was no way to make this asshole understand. There was no way he and his department were going to be able to find her daughter.

Glancing out the door she saw Tenny appear in the hallway. Carter's heart skipped a beat the way it always did when she saw her ex-lover. Standing still outside the office in her jeans and cowgirl boots, the gun hidden by her folded arms but not the glimmering badge which she proudly displayed. Tenny's dark hair was pulled loosely back into a short ponytail, so that her sharp cheekbones seemed to provide an even more intense stare. Not even the bandages and bruises could distract from her beauty. Although she had not said a word yet, her presence was already making a difference. Carter's spirits rose slightly and she sat up straight with a hint of a smirk on her lips as she looked directly into the idiot's eyes.

He was still going on about her ex-husband, not realizing anybody else was listening. His back was to the door. "Look, I think I've danced around the subject enough. We've determined that your ex-husband knows about your sexual orientation. Even though you claim that he's comfortable with it, that may have just been a ploy to relax you, to get you to trust him. I can't imagine that he would want his daughter brought up in the environment that you and your . . . girlfriend create."

Tenny had heard enough. As the detective continued placing the blame on Carter she walked into the office uninvited and stood behind Carter's chair, resting her hands on Carter's shoulders. The other detective stopped speaking when he saw Tenny. He obviously knew who she was. Her reputation as "ice woman" preceded her.

"Excuse me, Mr. Reese. . ." Tenny started, but was immediately interrupted.

"That's Detective Reese and I believe you are Detective Mendoza?"

"I am, but I think I'll stick to Mr. Reese for you, because you obviously aren't any kind of investigator. Sitting there letting your own prejudices interfere with a child-abduction investigation."

Tenny could see that this one had a temper. The veins in his neck began to poke out as his face flushed. She could almost see his slow mind working as he decided whether or not to take her on and defend himself.

He bolted from the chair and stood in front of Tenny,

poking his finger in her face. "Look here, I don't know who the fuck you think you are, but this is my investigation and you can just get the hell out!"

Tenny smiled, anticipating what Reese was about to experience. She didn't need him, but Steve enjoyed coming to the rescue occasionally.

Detective Reese's face paled quickly as Steve's huge hand clasped onto his shoulder and started to squeeze as he dragged Reese back and down into his chair. Reese looked up. Tenny smiled to herself. Steve was Herculean, standing over Reese. His chest was the size of an oak barrel and his arms as thick as the legs on most people. Tenny knew he was really harmless, but he could easily convince others of his danger.

"I'm Sergeant Steve Carson and you're out-of-line, asshole. You may want to be nicer to the detectives who are loaned to this department under the abduction protocol."

"I didn't activate the protocol for this fucking investigation. It's a simple case of child-stealing by a parent."

Tenny lashed out. "Of course you didn't activate it, you haven't got enough brains for that — I did. Right now our other partner is walking your captain through the process. The captain was a little perturbed to find out that a county protocol has been in existence for over a year and your department still doesn't have its own written policy in place. Who was responsible for that, Reese?"

Reese's anger appeared to evaporate as he sat back and took a deep breath. Yet under his breath he protested, "It's just a waste of time."

Tenny stood Carter up and moved her toward the door as Steve stepped to the side. Tenny responded in a tone that was so cool it was condescending. "By the way, my department has assigned four investigators per the protocol and I'll be the lead. But since you like to ignore things, you can just ignore us. We'll just handle the mundane stuff while you solve this case by locating Brian, her ex."

Tenny escorted Carter from the office as Reese feebly interjected, "Hey, we weren't done."

"Looks like you are now." Steve casually strolled out of the office.

In the hall they met with Ashley who was walking with a woman and speaking intently. Ashley smiled as she introduced her. "This is Captain Wilkins."

The captain shook everybody's hand and reassured Carter. "Now, if you'll excuse me I need to have a few words with Detective Reese." She walked down to his office and closed the door.

Steve shook his head. "A closed door . . . uh, not a good sign."

Tenny was agitated. "He ignored a county policy regarding child abductions, which requires him to activate the protocol in a certain time limit. He could have had help from every agency in this county within minutes." Tenny was becoming angry and tried to relax. "But because he assumed it was a parental abduction we lost valuable time. Look, I'm going to take Carter home. Do you guys mind staying here and making sure that the basics get covered?"

"No problem. We'll get them on the right track and meet you at home later." Ashley paused for a second and then gave Tenny one of her sly smiles. "Even though Los Palos is not in this county, I convinced them to let us stay and assist for the next few days. I told them it would be good experience in case we ever had an abduction. It looks like it's the three of us again."

Tenny hid her pleasure and sarcastically jabbed, "Maybe this time you two amateurs can keep up."

* * * * *

23

Tenny got all the information she needed from Carter as they drove. Carter hadn't heard anything unusual but noticed a small blue compact making a quick corner as she walked out of the house. At first Carter thought Kelsey was hiding from her, but then after several minutes she realized something was seriously wrong. She called the police immediately, but the first responding officers had taken about half an hour before they too decided that there was really a violation.

Tenny recognized the guilt and frustration that Carter felt as she began to cry. Tenny took her hand and looked at her. She was going to say something to comfort Carter, but what do you tell a woman who's just lost a child? Left to deal with the fact that her daughter had been taken from right under her nose, she was as much a victim as Kelsey. Tenny squeezed Carter's hand and tried to make herself believe that things were going to be all right.

When they reached the house, Carter's girlfriend was waiting, having rushed home from a business trip. Tenny and the new girlfriend didn't really get along, so she didn't offer to come in. "I'll give you a call later on." Carter nodded and slowly exited the car.

For a moment she turned to Tenny as if to ask for more, but then she was in her girlfriend's arms. Tenny quickly drove away.

Tenny tried not to let her mind wander as she drove home, wanting to think about the steps which needed to be taken for the investigation. But her thoughts kept straying to memories of Kelsey. Sharing Carter's love had not been easy for either of them at first. Tenny had often caught herself being extremely jealous of the three-year-old, and felt like a child herself for reacting that way. There were confrontations, power struggles for attention and tantrums, with Tenny always trying to remind herself that she was the adult.

It had taken months before Tenny was willing to try to deal with the child on her own. But every time she was left alone with Kelsey they would have major scenes, especially when it was time for her to go to bed. Kelsey would not sleep until her mom was there to put her to bed. It was as if she was afraid that if she went to sleep before her mother came home, she wouldn't see her again. Nothing could comfort Kelsey, and nothing could make Tenny understand why the child didn't trust her.

Then finally, one night when Carter was meeting with Brian, Tenny was so tired that she didn't even try to get Kelsey to bed. Instead she went into Kelsey's bedroom and crawled between the Little Mermaid quilt and the Little Mermaid sheets. She pulled a Little Mermaid pillow under her head and closed her eyes. Within a few minutes she felt a small body snuggling up against her.

"You're in my bed."

"I know, but I'm sleepy and it looked like a safe place to be."

"My mommy and you make it safe. Read me a story."

"How about if I just tell you one."

The child liked that idea and snuggled closer. Within minutes they were both asleep. From that moment on, Tenny had felt like she truly belonged not only in Carter's life but in Kelsey's too. That belief had never left Tenny. No matter what the circumstances were she knew that she would always have some place in their lives. For now, her place was in the search.

Chapter Three

The air grew cooler and woke her from a troubled sleep. The comforter on which she lay was old and smelled of dog, sweaty humans and urine. But it was soft and her only warmth, so she dug in deeper and once again started to cry quietly. The inside of the van was now completely dark and Kelsey decided that it must be night. That would mean that by now her mom would be looking for her.

Kelsey wasn't really scared anymore, but tears continued to roll down her cheeks. She missed her mom, her home and her bed. But the man hadn't been mean to her, not even when she was crying and asking for her mom. In fact, he hadn't said anything to her the entire time, except for when they switched from the car to this van. Then he had just told her to get in the back and he shut the door behind her. Kelsey had thought to fight or try to get away, but when they had switched to the van they were out in the middle of the country somewhere. She was as afraid of being out there alone as she was of being with him.

All the warnings of strangers trying to steal children came flooding into her mind, but nobody ever explained what happened once you were taken. She knew it was a bad thing, but she had no idea what to fear.

Her friends had always told stories about strangers taking children and then hacking them into pieces, but she hadn't seen any tools of mayhem. She comforted herself by reasoning that her friends didn't know anything. They had never been taken.

Kelsey rolled to her back so that she could breathe the stale air in the van, which was better than breathing directly into the blanket. The tears slowed as she forced herself to think good thoughts. After all, by this time her mother had probably told the police what had happened and they would be helping in the search. Kelsey remembered what Elizabeth had told her about the good guys always winning. Police officers were the good guys and Kelsey was confident that they would find her. In fact, she was sure that they were on their way to get her right now and take her home. Then the three of them would be together again. Thoughts of them all being a family again ended Kelsey's tears and she drifted back to sleep.

The van's leaving the paved roadway jolted Kelsey from sleep. It rocked and bounced downhill on what Kelsey could only guess was a dirt road filled with potholes. The sound of soft dirt soon became a slosh of mud. They eventually came to a stop.

For a moment there was nothing but silence and her own heavy breathing. Soon the driver's door creaked a painful moan as it was forced open. Then the door was viciously slammed. Kelsey heard the man walk around the van, but then there was more silence. Maybe her friends had been right. Maybe this was the time that he was going to cut her into small pieces and scatter her all around. Kelsey began to cry again, but this time the quiet tears turned to sobs. Fear spread throughout her body and each muscle which it touched began to tremble.

The back door to the van was yanked open and a steady bright beam blinded her. She couldn't see what was hidden behind the light and pushed herself up against the far side of the van. There was no escape.

"It's okay, baby, everything is going to be fine. You're safe now."

It wasn't her mother's voice, but the woman's voice sounded so much like her mom's that Kelsey began to feel as if her journey was over and she could go home.

The woman climbed into the back of the van and closed the door behind her. "Hi there. What's your name?" She spoke tenderly as she touched Kelsey's face.

"Kelsey."

"Oh, that's a pretty name and you're a pretty girl. I'm Doctor Jenkins and I'm going to take care of you now until we can get you where you belong. That man who took you didn't hurt you at all, did he?"

"No."

Gently the doctor pulled Kelsey to her and began to lift her shirt and check her for injuries. "Did he touch you anywhere that your clothing covers?"

"No, he's not suppose to, that's what my mommy says."

"Yes, and your mommy's right. She'd be happy to know that you listen." The doctor wrapped a nice clean blanket around Kelsey and lifted her from the van. Once out in the night, Kelsey realized that there were no police with uniforms and cars with red and blue lights like Elizabeth had. Instead, there was the man who had tricked her and another older man standing next to the van. A few feet away was a nice big white sedan that was clean and shiny, like new.

The woman walked over to the car which was still running and gently placed Kelsey in the back seat.

Kelsey watched the woman walk back to the two men. "Go ahead and pay him, she's perfect."

A large amount of cash was exchanged, then the younger man got back into the van and left without a word. The couple walked back to the car and got inside.

"She's just right. Do you think we can do this without changing her appearance? Our customers would prefer her the way she is right now," the woman said. "She's perfect."

The man sounded confident. "Sure, the paperwork shouldn't be too hard since this is our fourth one with them. It should just be a matter of a few weeks. I think that if we get a few more states between us and her mother we'll be fine. We'll put her at a safe house in the meantime and tell them to keep her out of sight."

He started to drive back up the bumpy road, but the advanced suspension on the luxury sedan allowed Kelsey to ignore what had been jolts in the van. The heater was on, the car was so warm, the blanket so soft and the woman was so gentle that Kelsey was asleep before they reached the highway.

Chapter Four

The portable trailer was parked in the police department's lot where it had been set up the morning after the abduction. It was crowded with desks, telephones and computers. Wires were strewn about the floor, running this way and that. The whole room viewed from above would give the impression of a microchip examined closely through a magnifying glass. The trailer had been staffed with a dozen detectives from surrounding agencies and a troop of volunteers provided by a nonprofit organization for missing children. The pace of the investigation had been hectic for several days, but with no new leads or clues, the multi-agency investigation had come to an end.

At first the focus had been on locating Carter's ex-husband, Brian. Although Tenny had argued vehemently against this diversion, she had lost to the traditional law enforcement philosophy of starting with the basics. Most abductions were by parents, but Tenny knew better in this case. Valuable time had been sacrificed in the first few days until Brian was located on his Caribbean vacation. Carter had known he was on vacation in the Caribbean but hadn't known his itinerary. Even when confirmation had been made of his whereabouts and he immediately headed for home, suspicion remained until he arrived at the department and told everybody exactly what he thought of their theory. He loved his ex-wife and supported her in her lifestyle. He loved his daughter even more and he expected them to find her.

Tenny had led the volunteers assigned to follow up on the blue car. Their investigation revealed that there were seven outstanding stolen vehicles that matched the description provided by Carter. Again Reese became focused on only those vehicles and assigned a special crime scene evidence team to be sent out each time one was recovered. When Tenny requested that the volunteers start checking with the individual police agencies for reports of abandoned vehicles, Detective Reese had told her it was a time-consuming exercise in futility.

Tenny was left to check the computer each day for vehicles which had been towed as abandoned, and at last she had found the car. It had been towed from Napa County, where it was found stripped and burned on a quiet country road. The sheriff's deputy told Tenny that the car was intact when he tagged it as abandoned, but by the time he went back a few days later it had been destroyed. He sounded surprised and explained that stuff like that didn't happen in these parts. Tenny didn't bother to clue him in on the significance of the car. The destruction of evidence must have been an afterthought for the suspect.

Their best lead was gone due to Reese's inability to conduct a thorough investigation. Tenny didn't share the information that she had discovered with him. He would only find a way to reduce the importance of it, especially because any value it would have provided was lost, destroyed by well-paid vandals.

The telephones had stopped ringing and the trail had grown cold. Tenny sat with one leg up on the corner of a desk and stared at a phone. She knew that Kelsey wouldn't have gone voluntarily. There had to have been some type of struggle. The suspect couldn't have gotten out of the area that quickly without attracting some attention. It was hard for her to believe that nobody out there had seen anything. She was sure that somebody had witnessed an important clue but rationalized away their own suspicions. Tenny wanted them to pick up the phone and tell her what they saw. She could determine if it was important or not. That was her job.

Steve and Ashley sat at the other end of the trailer and watched her. The abduction occurred in Carlmont, so Reese had the lead in this investigation. Without control, Tenny felt useless. Frustration had been all that the three detectives could offer as they obediently performed the tasks assigned to them.

A taxi pulled up to the trailer. Steve and Ashley weren't ready to leave, but outside assistance was no longer needed and their own department had plenty of cases waiting.

Ashley stood. "The cab's here..." Tenny could tell she wanted to say more, but what was left to say? The investigation had failed. Tenny watched as the tears of disappointment trickled from Ashley's eyes. Grabbing her bag, Ashley left the trailer. No strength left for a good-bye.

Steve slowly crossed the trailer and squatted behind Tenny's chair. He wrapped his heavy arms around her and rested his head on her uninjured shoulder. The unshaven stubble of a beard scratched at her cheek as she leaned her head against his.

"We can stay. We can get a flight later tonight so that we're here when you're done talking to Carter."

Tenny touched the scars around his hand and thought that at one time the three of them had been unbeatable. "I'll be fine."

He gave her a gentle squeeze. "This isn't your fault. You can't protect everybody. Something will break. They'll find her."

"They won't find her." In an instant the anger was gone, replaced by sorrow. "What will I tell Carter? How do I look her in the eye and tell her that she won't get to watch Kelsey grow up, won't hear her laughter again, won't feel her hug, won't wipe away her tears? How do I do that?"

Steve kissed her cheek and stood to leave. "You don't, Tenny. All the knowledge of her loss is in her, just like it's inside you. You won't have to tell her anything — but that you tried."

"It's not as if the cops really care anyway."

This comment stopped Tenny in mid-sentence. Carter's lover, Blair, had been antagonistic from the moment Tenny arrived. The interruptions while Tenny tried to explain about the investigation had been annoying and inappropriate. But this last comment was all she was going to take.

Carter moved from her chair to the couch next to Tenny as the two women silently stared at each other. Tenny was ready to unleash her frustration and anger with

33

a chilling combination of berating comments. Then she felt Carter's hand on her leg.

A soft squeeze of communication, indicating that Carter knew Tenny was on the edge.

"Elizabeth cares." Carter looked at Blair as she offered a recension of her lover's hurtful statement.

"Oh yeah, she cares, but not about Kelsey."

The conversation was getting out of control. Tenny wouldn't take this immature behavior for much longer. She had already tolerated enough out of respect for the situation.

Carter's tone was sharp, maybe defensive. "Will you please leave! I want to talk to Elizabeth by myself."

After a long moment of uncomfortable silence, Blair stood and marched from the room. Tenny and Carter both sighed with relief.

"Why do you put up with her?" Tenny would never understand what Carter saw in the woman.

"I don't want to get into that." Carter turned to Tenny.

She seemed so spiritless, Tenny thought, as if each day that passed without her daughter sucked a little more life from her body. Tenny couldn't find the joy and sensuality that always roared from Carter's deep brown eyes. Instead there was only emptiness. A strange appearance of confusion, loneliness and fear. This woman had always had somebody to love and to love her no matter what. She had her daughter.

"Tenny, I know that she's out there somewhere waiting for her mommy to come get her. I know she's not dead. I'm not going to give up, but there's not much I can do. I wouldn't even know where to begin." Carter stopped awkwardly.

Clearly unable to look at Tenny, she tumbled the ring on her finger. It was the ring that Tenny had given her on their anniversary.

"I saw you on television in that special about your rape investigation. I was so proud of you. I know how important it is to you to take little pieces of what's wrong in this world and make them right." She hesitated. "Now I need you to help me. I know why everybody calls you Tenacity. I know it's you that can bring my baby home."

Tenny couldn't stand to sit still any longer. The word *home* launched her from the couch and followed her as she paced the living room. This place was not home. Tenny didn't belong here, but Kelsey's and Carter's home should have been with Tenny. None of this made any sense. What was she doing here? This was a part of her life which was over.

Tenny stopped at the front window and took several deep breaths, trying to focus her thoughts. She had let her work take control of her life for many years. While she had been earning her nickname, she had been losing Carter. It was why Carter refused to call her Tenny. Her return to patrol after the rape investigation had been an attempt to be less driven. It was an agreement that she had made with herself to try and recapture some of the joy in her own life.

Tenny glanced at the fireplace mantel. It wasn't that she was looking for something in particular, she was just trying to get her bearings. On the mantel, turned toward Tenny, was the same picture of Carter and Kelsey that she had in her own house. She took two steps and lifted the picture from its place. As she held their photograph, the memory of her promise filled her turbulent mind.

Tenny didn't really fit in the little child's swing, but Kelsey had insisted that she sit there so Kelsey could sit on her lap and they could swing together. The metal pieces strapping the thick nylon together were digging into

Tenny's back and thighs, the swing angrily complaining that she was too big for its small frame. After about twenty minutes, the child had finally had enough. As they had gently moved in tiny circles, Tenny fought off the last remnants of motion sickness.

Kelsey had become intrigued by their conversation and had lost interest in the lifts, speed and feeling of flight, but she refused to relinquish her spot on Tenny's lap. They sat, barely in motion, and spoke of their own special family.

Kelsey had been at the age when she was beginning to realize that her home was different from that of the other kids at her nursery school. None of the other kids had an Elizabeth that slept with their mommy. Kelsey understood that Elizabeth wasn't a boy, but the other kids' mommies had boyfriends or daddies that slept with them. She had tried introducing Elizabeth as mommy's boyfriend, but nobody ever seemed to understand. People always corrected her, while Elizabeth stood by with an embarrassed smile. She had tried calling Elizabeth Daddy, but that wasn't right either. She had a daddy.

So as they huddled together in the swing, she asked Tenny questions about how they were a family. Every time Tenny gave an answer, Kelsey dug deeper. She probably could sense better than any adult how much Tenny cared for people and how much love was inside her. Finally the quest for undying love had come in the form of yet another question.

"What if somebody takes me away some day?"

"Nobody's going to take you away, babe." Tenny gave her a small kiss on the head to reassure her.

"But what if somebody does?" Kelsey would not let Tenny avoid the question.

"Then I'll find you and bring you back."

"But what if they hide me, or dress me up different so you can't find me?"

Tenny could sense the child working herself into an actual state of fear. "I'll still find you."

"But how?"

Tenny pointed to the birthmark on the child's neck. It had always embarrassed Kelsey, but Tenny gave it a new significance. "This birthmark tells the world that you belong to your mommy, daddy and me. Nobody will ever be able to change this and no matter where somebody may take you, or how they may hide you, I will always be able to find you. I just have to look for this mark."

Finally Kelsey had been satisfied.

Tenny set the picture down and started for the door. "I'll find her. I promise."

Chapter Five

The child was discreetly secluded in the safe house
near Miami. Theresa's home was the safe house of
preference because law enforcement agencies in the state of
Florida were overburdened by the problems created by
hurricanes, illegal immigration, drug smuggling and violent
street crime. These officials had no idea that their fine
state had also become a holding ground for abducted
children who were awaiting deportation.

It wasn't the police Theresa feared — it was the
parents. Theresa was herself a mother and she knew that
a mother was something to fear. A mother. would not sleep
at night. She would not maintain a normal routine. She
would not think of anything else, never giving up. It was

the parents of missing children that organized the constant reminders in the mail, in the newspapers and on milk cartons. They didn't have to worry about the next crime. They wouldn't stop until they found their children. Theresa knew that was why the Jenkinses had brought this girl all the way to her. They could afford it. The international sales of abducted children had become an extremely profitable business for the Jenkinses. There were several countries where the wealthy who were unable to conceive children themselves were also unable to adopt children that met their standards. The contradicting traditions of being a melting pot and of cultural diversity in the United States served to provide the perfect hunting ground for children meeting the specifications of their customers. In the U.S.A. a child of any racial, religious and/or cultural makeup could be found. Plus the country's health care system, although often criticized, still served to make American children some of the healthiest in the world.

Tom Jenkins's international legal consulting practice provided the perfect cover for him and allowed him to bribe officials throughout the world in order to obtain the necessary forms. When the children left the States, all their adoption papers were always in perfect order. In addition, his wife's medical practice assured their customers that the children they received were healthy and had all the necessary shots for their travels.

Theresa had been a special find for the Jenkinses. She was a registered nurse and had just been laid off when their paths crossed. Theresa needed the money and they had plenty to give her. All she had to do was care for one extra child every once in a while. Theresa didn't really know where the children went. But she did know that they would be treated well. This permitted her to deceive herself, and to reason that whatever was happening couldn't be that bad. Most importantly, it was paying for her new house on the coast and putting food on her table.

The child brought to her on the last day of September was a beauty. Her skin was a smooth white cream which would brown easily in the warmth of the sun. Her eyes were a deep brown that Theresa guessed would appear to grow darker with the child's skin. She was also sure that the child had a magical smile, although she had not seen it. Kelsey — that was the child's name — didn't seem sad but she never smiled.

The child seemed content as she politely followed instructions. She didn't ask a hundred questions like the others. There was not the daily inquiry about her parents or where she was, or where she was going. Instead Kelsey patiently went about her days, filling them with quiet songs. Theresa sensed that the child was waiting, as if her mother was simply late in retrieving her from school.

Theresa sat down next to the child in the sun as she hummed a tune and drew the ocean with crayons. "Do you know why you're here?"

The child looked at her as if that was a silly question. "Because they took me from my mommy."

Her blunt statement of the truth made Theresa uncomfortable. Why was she so calm? She wanted to ask, but she felt as if she wouldn't like the answer. However, the child continued, providing the information Theresa sought.

Kelsey spoke as if Theresa should have known. "It's all right though because I have the mark of love and Elizabeth will be coming for me." Kelsey pointed to the birthmark on her neck and then went back to her picture.

Theresa stood and looked again at Kelsey. In that instant she decided that this would be the last time she concealed a child. She was glad the week was almost over. Something suddenly felt dangerous.

Chapter Six

"I realize that, sir. You know I wouldn't have asked if I didn't really need the time off." Tenny had spent thirty minutes patiently listening to the lieutenant complain about staffing levels and reminding her that her request didn't conform to department policies on vacation selection. He had to make sure Tenny understood what a big favor he was doing for her. He wanted her to know that she would owe him something. The lieutenant would settle for a little more respect. "Of course, sir, I know this wasn't easy for you. Thanks so much for your help."

Tenny hung up the phone. She had a week's worth of vacation. But she had no idea how long her search would take. It could be years.

"Shit, I have to start somewhere."

Tenny grabbed her green bomber jacket off the chair and headed out the door. The investigation had provided no clues. There was no place to begin. No leads left to follow. Tenny was going to the only starting point she knew.

The huge concrete building was supposed to look modern but it appeared intimidating. Institutional, cold, harsh academia. It had been built not to encourage socialization but to stimulate learning. Free the mind from all distractions, including interesting architecture, and force it to concentrate on the task. The accumulation of knowledge.

Tenny's heart began to pound as she entered. Libraries represented the ultimate. All the answers to each question were hidden among the words which were spread throughout this one building. The challenge was to frame the question correctly, collect the knowledge and then piece the words and their meanings together in just the right way to reveal the answer. In these pages were all the facts, data and information the world needed. The key was the willingness to learn. Tenny was here to learn.

Libraries were nothing new for Tenny. She remembered the endless days of research and reading while she completed her graduate education. The degree didn't really indicate that she had become a master of the field. Instead it symbolized her domination of the skill to collect information from multiple sources, then mold that information into some type of recommendation, policy or program. An ability to create a solution.

The computer terminals were full so Tenny walked over to the periodicals, quickly scanned the different reference indexes. She selected the 1969 social science listings. She flipped through the pages, checking the various combinations of headings that might divulge the information she sought, but she found nothing. Child abduction — nothing. Child stealing — nothing. Kidnapping — nothing about children. Reluctantly she checked Homicide — thankfully nothing specifically about children.

Apparently child abduction was a more recent criminal phenomenon, but Tenny continued her search year by year. She didn't want to miss anything. Not one small clue. After a few hours of standing quietly among the books that provide the first hints, Tenny had compiled an extensive list of articles. She headed upstairs.

The aisles of bound literature, the maze of published material, this is where the trail begins, Tenny thought. It was among these rows of printed words that Tenny hoped to piece together the frame of the puzzle, which eventually would reveal Kelsey. The aisles were long and narrow, stretching across the building's belly. The shelves reached almost to the ceiling, with the closely packed books obscuring the light from the next artery.

Tenny found her first group of bound articles and as she pulled the book from the shelf, she was drawn to the bright red covers above her. *Child Psychology,* embossed in gold, loomed above her. Tenny smiled and recalled the last time she had been drawn here in search of answers. Blushing as she recalled her past indiscretions, she looked up and down the aisle as if it was all about to happen again.

She had dragged Carter to the library. Carter didn't believe in learning from books, she learned from living. Always pushing herself and those around her to fit as much living as possible into each day. Always trying new things, asking new questions and approaching life from new directions. But this time the questions were not about Carter's life, they were about her daughter's, and Carter didn't want to risk the mistakes that life can often bring. Therefore Tenny had talked her into coming to the library and reading about what they might expect trying to raise Kelsey together.

Of course, Carter wasn't about to let their quest be another mundane trip to the library.

Carter had snatched the reference number from Tenny's hand and sprinted up the stairs ahead of her. When Tenny reached the third floor, Carter was nowhere in sight. Tenny began to walk, peering down each aisle, hoping to glimpse her lover. As she passed by the S-X row she observed Carter peeking around the end of the bookshelves. Instantly Carter was gone, but her giggling echoed through the silent cavern of academia. Tenny was immediately consumed by the chase and darted after Carter, forgetting her surroundings.

Reaching the end of the row, Tenny looked in the direction that Carter had gone. Standing about seven columns away, Carter was facing Tenny as she casually leaned against the shelf. With her shoulder propped against the shelf, she had both hands shoved not into her pockets, but down the front of her jeans with the first button innocently unfastened. There was a lustful smirk on her face; it was a tease that caused Tenny to look around her to ensure nobody else was being invited by this sensual woman. Tenny took a step toward her, and Carter again disappeared among the stacks.

This time, though, Tenny did not pursue. Instead she stepped down a different aisle. Two could play at this game. Sauntering along, trying to act as if she was interested in the books, Tenny waited for her lover to come looking. After a few moments, she heard a voice.

"I never knew libraries could be so interesting, so intriguing, so exciting." Then Carter began to make low,

44

soft moaning sounds. Tenny glanced up to see if she could just climb over the damn stack of books and drop down upon her lover.

"Damn." There wasn't enough space at the top. Tenny ran to the end of the aisle and lunged around the corner. Carter was seated on a stool about halfway down the aisle. Her arms were spread across the shelf behind her, while her legs were spread and resting up on the bookshelf across from her.

"I found the one you were looking for." Carter smiled coyly at Tenny.

"Really? And where might it be?" Tenny was moving forward slowly, speaking softly, not wanting to spook her prey again.

"It's right here between my legs." Carter innocently pointed at the bookshelves, but her statement didn't need clarification.

"Well, what did it say?" Tenny was almost close enough to touch her, and the throbbing throughout her body was making it difficult to concentrate on her apprehension of this flaunting flirt.

"It said that all we have to do is love each other."

Carter reached out and latched on to Tenny, wrapping her legs around her. Tenny wanted to protest. She wanted to point out that they were in a public library, but Carter's lips were on her own before she could voice her concerns. The moment their lips touched, Tenny's prudishness was sucked from her.

The photocopies of articles, studies and testimonies were spread across the kitchen table and scattered about the floor. She had been up since early morning — day two of her search. After reading everything once, she had gone back through them and highlighted information in different

45

pastel colors. Light blue indicated information on numbers and locations of abductions. Pink signified age, sex, race and other information about the victims. Yellow identified any possible suspect information. Orange denoted any theories of the way abductions occurred or why. Finally, green marked the names of researchers and "experts" in the field.

Next Tenny had gone through the articles again, cutting them apart and reorganizing the information in her new color-coded system. Then she had reviewed the stacks of highlighted pieces one last time, searching for the one clue that would help her to find Kelsey. But now as Tenny stared at all the information, anticipation evolved into frustration. She had expected to find so much more than was there. Only about twenty articles discussed child abduction in general. Thus Tenny had been forced to collect articles of actual abductions from local newspapers and try to piece together her own conclusions.

What Tenny discovered was that media attention focused on child-stealing and abductions reached its peak in the early 1980s with growing statistics causing much alarm and stimulating moderate responses from the government. A few laws were passed to help control parental child-stealing, and the FBI promised to research stranger abductions. But then in 1987 the concern for this problem took a drastic swing in the other direction. Several FBI researchers and independent sociologists began to dispute the accuracy of prior reports of the number of children who were victims. The "experts" began to use words and phrases like *myths, social construction, misleading statistics* and *media sensationalism.* Some even went so far as to warn that society's preoccupation with child abduction was actually damaging to the children, who felt they could no longer be safe anywhere. By 1992 the subject had practically disappeared from the journals, magazines and texts.

Then in 1993 the topic came rushing back to the forefront when a young girl from Petaluma, California, was snatched from her home. The abduction was solved, but with a tragic ending which prompted changes in police practices and felony sentencing. Yet, the furor passed and children continued to disappear.

Tenny slammed her fists onto the table and shoved the mounds of paper to the floor. The anger exploded as she thought of Kelsey out there somewhere, waiting to become another statistic. Why didn't people demand more? Why were people so willing to accept that some children would be taken each year and no one would ever know why?

Tenny marched out to the living room and tried to pace off her frustration. As she stormed in circles, caught in the eye of her own hurricane, Tenny began to focus on the magazines on her coffee table. She subscribed to all the news magazines and their covers answered her questions. They announced news of the economy, war in Europe, health care reform, AIDS and cancer, crime and civil unrest. Where did one person start?

Tenny knew where she was going to start. Except in a few cases, the children abducted by strangers appeared to be random. What was motivating so many strangers to steal children, and where were they? If they were all dying, why weren't more bodies discovered? The abductors actually apprehended were never really clear about their motives or why they picked the children they did. Some piece of important information was missing. She had only one more place where she might find it.

Betsy Hoffman had been the FBI's child abduction special investigator and headed their investigations for years. She was also Tenny's first lover. When Tenny started her career in law enforcement with the FBI she had been naïve and susceptible to idealism. She had found in Betsy her own protector as she entered the strange and controversial worlds of law enforcement and homosexuality. She and Betsy had been lovers for about six months, then Tenny had been reassigned to the Atlanta office. The distance had ended their affair but not their love for each other. Betsy had been Tenny's teacher, mentor, protector, lover and friend. It was the friendship that would last for both. It was the friendship that Tenny counted on as she dialed Betsy's number.

Betsy sounded groggy, slow, sleepy. Tenny glanced at the clock and realized that it was 10:00 PM. She hadn't even noticed that it was dark outside.

"Shit, girl, I just looked at the clock. What is it there, midnight?"

Betsy laughed. "Don't worry, Elizabeth. I've read that as you get older you don't need as much sleep, so you're actually doing me a favor."

Betsy was another person that refused to use Tenny's nickname. Betsy thought that there was enough self-inflicted pressure, she didn't need to try to live up to somebody else's misguided naming.

"Before you tell me why you called, is this going to require a cup of coffee?"

Tenny knew that Betsy couldn't think straight without a certain amount of caffeine in her system. "Better make a pot."

"Shit. What's the problem?" Betsy's tone grew serious.

Tenny described the events of the last week and a half, explaining her frustration with the formal investigation and the steps which she had taken on her own. She went over the information that her research had revealed. Then she asked for help.

"Look, dear, I know how much you're hurting. God knows I've seen enough families of missing children. But you can't make this your personal battle . . . I mean, search.

I spent a career looking and I just came up empty in the end."

Tenny hadn't missed the small slip in Betsy's word selection. She had to make Betsy understand that this was her battle, or search, or life. She had made a promise that she intended to keep. "Betsy, I'm not going to walk away this time. I'm not going to turn my back and ignore the problem that's right in front of my face. I am not giving up!"

Betsy's voice was gentle. "Tenny, what happened to Pearl was not your fault."

"Oh bullshit, don't give me that therapist crap. I was standing right there with her hours before she died. She reached out to me and I ignored her. All I had to do to save them was insist that they come with me, that's all. But I didn't. I turned and I walked away, knowing it was the wrong thing to do. Don't tell me it wasn't my fault!" Tenny was on the verge of tears.

Betsy tried to soothe her. "Babe, the case was never solved, we don't know why Pearl was killed or what happened to the children. They were on the streets, running from danger. It might have happened anyway."

The anger erupted. "That's right. I never solved the case. I couldn't even find the answers to why!"

"Damn it, Elizabeth, there's nothing you could have done. I was there too, remember. We assisted your investigation and there was nothing the FBI could have done. It went way beyond the simple street crime. What happened would have happened days later. You couldn't protect them forever."

Soon after the investigation into Pearl's death and the abduction of her grandchildren Betsy had suddenly retired from the FBI. Now she was teaching full time in Minnesota. The explanation for her quick retirement was that after the last presidential election, things had gotten kind of hot in the Federal Bureau, which didn't have much tolerance for her sexual orientation. The new president, a Democrat, had excited many gays and lesbians, inducing them to step from their closets. But at the same time, actual change among the nation's policies was slow to occur, leaving many at the mercy of their individual employers. Betsy had been one of the unfortunates.

Tenny had really never accepted that explanation. Betsy was too good at what she did to be sacrificed solely for her sexual orientation. Anyway, Betsy was never shy about her taste and the Bureau must have known her preferences for years. There was something more to Betsy's departure, but Tenny had never pushed her for the truth. Now there was a long silence.

Tenny was calm as she asked, "What do you know?"

"I didn't mean to keep this from you. I just didn't know if I should tell you. I mean, your life was already so difficult. You were so obsessed with what happened, I didn't want it to totally ruin what was left of your life."

Again, Tenny asked, "What do you know?"

"Pearl's oldest granddaughter, Angelica, is alive. She's in Portland, Oregon." Betsy paused, but Tenny did not respond. No gasp. No expression of shock. No questions. Nothing but silence as she waited for the explanation. Betsy was careful. "I was in Portland two years ago for an unrelated abduction investigation and I stumbled upon her."

Tenny knew that you don't just stumble onto missing children, but she didn't want to interrupt. She wanted to know about Angelica.

"She was living in the streets. But she wasn't like the others. She was like Pearl, she respected herself. She was admirable in her homelessness, working hard for her shelter and food. The only help she asked for was from those that would take a few minutes and help her to learn. Teach her something, anything, as long as she didn't already know it." Betsy paused again. "I found her when she was fourteen. She had changed her last name so that her mother couldn't find her, or so she claimed. It took me several days to get the truth about her identity from her. She never did tell me what had happened except that her grandmother and sister were dead."

Tenny sensed Betsy's nervousness as she continued to listen in complete silence.

"I got Angelica into a private school in Portland which has year-round boarding for a few students. I also convinced her to briefly attend therapy, but Angelica's refusal to discuss the past left the therapist with little to do. Angelica's strength is remarkable. She's an excellent student and seems to be well-adjusted." Betsy stopped.

Finally Tenny spoke, her efforts to hold back the surge of tears making her voice a whisper. "Why did she trust you? Why did she let you help?"

Betsy began to cry. "I told her that I was your friend. Her grandmother had told her she could always trust Officer Mendoza, so she trusted me."

The confusion of emotions fused inside of Tenny and burst from her in her body's only way to express its sorrow and its happiness. The tears rained freely from Tenny. Unclear whether it was pain or joy, Tenny didn't know how to feel. "You should have told me."

"I couldn't."

Chapter Seven

This was not a city. It was a town. Maybe Tenny really was lost. She was supposed to be in Portland, but this couldn't be Portland. The houses had huge yards. There were no sidewalks. There wasn't even heavy traffic. She was sure she was in a rural town, somewhere far from Portland. In fact, she couldn't help but watch for cows along the roadway.

This was nothing like the Bay Area. Where were all the people? Where were all the cars? Where was she? Tenny pulled off the road again and looked at the map the rental car agency had provided. According to the map she was close to downtown.

"How could that be?" Tenny wondered aloud. She had

already taken one wrong turn as she left the airport. That mistake had taken her far out of the way before she discovered her error. Glancing at her watch, Tenny didn't have time for another extemporaneous tour of the area.

One more quick check of the map and Tenny pulled back onto the road and continued in what she hoped was the right direction. She entered a forested area and was almost ready to stop again, convinced that she was going the wrong way, when downtown Portland sprang into view below.

It was cradled tenderly between the gentle, green rise of the hills and the shimmering, slow-moving water of the Wiliamette River. A clean sharp image of skyscrapers jutting into softly falling mist and touching the tips of golden sun rays piercing a layer of clouds lay before her. A light layer of moisture cast over the entire landscape, causing it to sparkle.

Tenny drove into the downtown where her instructions to the boarding school began. The streets seemed empty, although it was a normal weekday morning. The sidewalks were clean, the buildings untouched by graffiti, and the people didn't look particularly hurried. Tenny rolled down her window. It even sounded quiet. She smiled. It was all so different from home. It was so . . . quaint.

Tenny turned toward the northwest section of town. As she drew closer to her destination, fascination gave way to stress. Tenny had left early in the morning after Betsy had promised to call the school and let them know that Tenny would be arriving to see Angelica. She had also warned Tenny that Angelica might not agree to see her, especially on such short notice. But Tenny knew there was a reason why she had found Angelica at this moment in their lives.

Tenny was confident, but as she pulled into the driveway of the school a sudden feeling of dread invaded. Could she face this child? The last time she had seen

Angelica, Pearl and her two granddaughters had been homeless. A crack-consumed mother had forced them out to the streets. Pearl defiantly continued to raise her grandchildren with more love, concern and guidance than many offered their children in the comfort of homes. With the help of Tenny and others in the community, Pearl had kept them in school, well-fed, clothed and safe. Her attitude had always been positive and she taught all those around her to appreciate what they did have in life, instead of desiring what they didn't. Tenny had admired this fine, tireless woman.

Looking up, Tenny noticed a tall, slim black girl standing still on the long porch of the school. Even from the distance, Tenny could tell that this young woman belonged to Pearl. The girl sat down on a damp step and waited, demonstrating to Tenny the patience that her grandmother had taught her so well.

Tenny released the pressure from the brake pedal and the car began to slowly coast forward. A dozen things to say ran through her mind as she pulled up to the steps. One sentence rejected after another. There were no words to articulate Tenny's tangled emotions. Yet her confidence returned and as she stepped from the car, Tenny knew that Pearl would send down the correct words, the proper movements, everything they would need.

As Tenny approached, Angelica held out a hand to her. The last time Tenny had been offered a hand from this family it had been in a quiet plea. Maybe even a good-bye from a woman who seemed to know the world so well. Tenny took her hand and they sat in silence as the sun finally fought off the mist and conquered the day.

* * * * *

54

Angelica had obtained her driver's license on her sixteenth birthday. Not because she ever expected to have the opportunity to use it. After all, she wouldn't be able to afford a car for years and she wasn't about to ask anybody to borrow theirs. But her license represented another test passed for Angelica. It told the world that she too knew how to drive a car and had performed the task with the necessary skill to become licensed. Angelica had not driven since the exam.

Tenny had been surprised at first to learn that Angelica had a license. But then she remembered what Betsy had told her about this child's need to learn everything. Without hesitation Tenny passed off the car keys to Angelica, who had accepted them as if they were treasure.

Angelica's time at school was spent studying and working. But when she did get a rare day to herself, she always headed out into the wilderness that surrounded the pioneering Portland. This time she drove them out along the Columbia River until they reached a park entrance.

When they stepped from the artificial silence of the auto, the peace and serenity of the earth's finer side instantly settled Tenny's frazzled nerves. All night she had tossed and turned as she debated what to say to Angelica. Now the sweet, crisp air cleared her muddled mind.

Tenny needed Angelica's help to find Kelsey. But this child seemed so at peace with her past, Tenny didn't want to risk bringing the pain back. She wanted to find a way to continue her search without Angelica. A way to make everything right for everybody with no more pain.

"So how did you find me?" Angelica had broken the silence as they climbed toward the top of the path.

"Betsy told me."

More silence, except for their heavy breathing as the path turned steeper. Tenny knew that Angelica wanted a more complete answer, but she still was not sure about how to proceed.

"Why did she tell you now, after all this time? I didn't ask her to." Tenny looked at Angelica's face, expecting to find some anger there. Instead, all that Tenny found was the intensity she was coming to know in this girl. Angelica didn't need anybody.

Tenny knew Kelsey depended on them both and that Angelica would be up to that responsibility. Maybe it was a chance for Angelica also. A chance to free herself from the past.

"I called Betsy for help. A small girl has been taken and I need to find her." Tenny watched Angelica for a reaction, a hint of what she was feeling inside. There was nothing. "She was stolen from in front of her house and all the leads that we had are gone now. I had no idea what to do so I called Betsy. She told me about you and something told me that I needed your help. It's an incredible long shot."

They arrived at the first viewing platform and Angelica broke from the path and walked to the railing. When she reached out to grasp the bar, Tenny saw all the pain. It burst from Angelica's clutch and exploded through her body as she grew tense. Asn they gazed at the falling water, the white sheet became the screen on which the suppressed images of Angelica's past came to life.

Tenny stepped close to her and after a moment placed her hand over Angelica's. Then, to Tenny's surprise, Angelica's hand came off the railing and began to squeeze Tenny's with an unreal strength.

"I wanted you to find us, but I knew you wouldn't. I knew that nobody would find us, because nobody would be looking." Angelica looked down at the ground as she spoke, as if embarrassed by her own honesty.

"I did look. I tried to find you and your grandmother's killer. But I wasn't good enough then. I followed procedures and stuck to the professional approach. I didn't trust my instincts, my feelings, my soul. I let my guilt interfere with my determination." Tenny paused and then said what she had been waiting for years to say. "I'm sorry."

Angelica began her trek up the path again. This time her pace had doubled. No longer was this a hike to the top of a mountain. Now it was a climb to evade the past.

Angelica spoke as she quickly moved forward. It was as if she believed she could shed the painful memories on the ground behind her and escape for good. "He shot her without even waking her first. I guess I've always been somewhat thankful for that. He just walked up in the middle of the night and shot her in the head. The shot woke us, but he moved my sister and me so fast from her arms that it wasn't until we were in the truck that I realized what had happened. I saw my grandmother's blood on my sister's head and knew that she was gone. But I'll never forget when the bullet struck. Her arms immediately tightened around us. He had trouble getting her to let go, even in her death. Of course I know now that it was just her body's natural reaction."

Tenny had to interrupt. "No, it wasn't, honey. It was her fighting to protect the two of you."

Angelica smiled slightly. "The man put us in the back of a truck with a camper shell and started to drive. The windows in the back were all covered so we couldn't see out and it was always pretty dark inside. We drove for a really long time and we just held each other the whole way. He stopped a few times and once he took my sister somewhere with him. Then finally we got to wherever and he blindfolded us and took us into this building."

They were almost to the top of the path and again it grew steeper, but Angelica's pace did not slow. Tenny felt as if she wanted to stop the girl. She didn't want to hear anymore.

"Inside the building there was a couple. He never took the blindfold off, but I heard their voices," Angelica explained. "I heard the woman say I was too old. Then she said she wanted to check the younger one and I heard her leave the room with my sister." Angelica took a deep breath. "A few moments later she came back and was really angry. She was screaming about him molesting her and therefore she wasn't acceptable either. The couple began to leave and the man who had taken us got enraged and asked what he was supposed to do with us now. The other man told him they didn't care what he did with us and they left. They just walked out the door and left us with him."

Finally they reached the highest viewing platform and Angelica stopped speaking for a moment. Although it was midday, Tenny felt a darkness surround them. Then the tears began to rush from Angelica as the water of the falls crashed down beneath them.

"He put us back in the truck and drove somewhere else. It wasn't too far. He stopped and came around to the back. He wanted my sister, but I wouldn't let her go. He was still so angry, I knew he was going to kill her. He punched me, but I still wouldn't let go. So he grabbed my fingers and started to break them one by one."

Tenny glanced at Angelica's hands and for the first time noticed the crooked and bent fingers. All ten of them.

"I tried to hang on, but I couldn't. He was too strong. He took her and put her up in the cab with him. I could hear her crying and him yelling at her. Then he said that he hadn't even fucked her and that doctor bitch rejected her. So now he was going to fuck her." Angelica began to open and close her fist as she continued. Tenny wanted to stop her, but it was too late. "I pounded on the glass between the cab and the back, but I couldn't break it. I screamed for him to stop, but he ignored me. I could feel the truck begin to rock back and forth and I knew what he was doing. I could hear my sister sobbing. The truck began to rock faster and faster. His grunting grew louder and louder. My sister's crying grew quieter and quieter. I know that she died with him on her. She just let herself escape into death." Angelica paused for a long moment. "I never saw her again. I never heard her voice again. I'm actually glad I never had to see her dead. But I know I heard her last breath."

Tenny was silent.

Angelica looked up at her. "When I heard that breath, it was as if she breathed her strength out for me to capture. My grandmother was gone. My sister was gone. But I was still there and I needed to finish their lives with my own. I decided I was going to fight and when he came to get me I was ready. I heard him at the tailgate and I was prepared to hurt him any way I could. As soon as I heard him unlatch it, I kicked with all my might. It hit him so hard that it knocked him down. I jumped out and began to run and I didn't stop. I ran until it was light outside and then I finally had the courage to turn and look to see if he was behind me. He wasn't and I was alone."

Tenny hadn't even realized that she too was crying. Finally she knew, and what she had heard terrified her. Tenny's stomach was twisting in fear. Kelsey was still out there and all of Tenny's instincts were telling her that these two kidnappings were related. She wanted Angelica to never have to think about this again, but she needed more.

"Angelica, you are such a brave girl. I can't even start to tell you how much I admire you. You will never be alone again, I promise. Thank you for telling me, but I have to ask you for more. Together we might be able to save another little girl." Tenny hesitated. "Will you tell me everything you remember about the man who took you and your sister?"

"Yes. But before I do I have to tell you something else."

Tenny waited, not knowing what to expect next.

"I know that you tried, just like I did to help my sister."

Tenny took Angelica into her arms and held her tight. "Thank you."

Chapter Eight

The wall against her back provided the only comfort as she impulsively searched the busy airport concourse for the suspect. Tenny knew that her suspect was a white male, probably in his early forties now. Angelica had described him as greasy and skinny. According to her he had a weary appearance that made him look ill. The most important information about him was that he had a large scar through his left eyebrow. In addition, on his right forearm he had a tattoo of a skull with a snake twisting through it.

Angelica could not provide any other information about the couple who had met with her abductor. After thinking on it forsix years she had concluded that the woman must have been a doctor, and Tenny agreed. Angelica had a good mind and an excellent sense of deduction. She had also reasoned that the couple must be quite powerful and dangerous, since the abductor took certain precautions to protect their identity which he had not bothered to take for himself.

Searching the face of every white male who walked by, Tenny could not get her mind to purge the image of this man killing Pearl. Habit pulled her right arm in close to her body to touch the gun she always wore on her hip. It wasn't there. The gun was at home because this was not an official investigation, and she didn't want the hassle with the airlines in order to carry her weapon on board.

Tenny dropped her shoulders and tried to relax. There was no danger here. The suspect was not in this airport. In fact, he was probably not even in this state. It was the airport itself that made her apprehensive. She could remember a time when she loved airports. They were an adventure in people-watching. That was before she had an airport confrontation with the most dangerous man in her career. He had almost taken Steve's life and had eluded her with the cleverness and sinister calmness that would haunt Tenny for the rest of her life. His presence now invaded every airport. Tenny realized that she had not really been searching the passersby for the suspect. It was him, Whittington, for whom she would always watch. The knowledge that he was serving a life sentence never really put her at ease.

Finally they called Tenny's flight for boarding and she began to focus on her current quest. There were hours of computer and telephone work ahead of her. She would use the rest of her vacation time if necessary, and if that wasn't enough, she would ask for a leave of absence.

Concentrating on her current case made her feel better, but she still waited until everybody else had boarded the plane before standing to join them. She didn't want anybody behind her.

The early flight out of Portland had Tenny back at the department by nine in the morning. She didn't even bother stopping by her house. There was too much work to do.

She went to the Records Division and found the supervisor. Although she didn't really know the man seated in the office, he had always been helpful with her questions in the past.

"Excuse me, Roy, do you have a minute to answer some questions for me?"

Roy looked up from his computer and smiled. "Of course, Detective, anything to help Ms. Tenacity. Please come in." He motioned her toward a chair next to his desk.

Tenny didn't want to mislead him. "Actually, I'm not in Investigations anymore. I'm back on the streets."

Roy nodded. "I know that, Detective, but you'll always be one of the best. You've earned the title for the rest of your career. In fact, with the attention you give to detail, I keep waiting for you to become the Records Coordinator."

Tenny had to look away. His honesty embarrassed her. "Well, thanks."

"So what's the question?" He probably sensed that he was making her uncomfortable.

"I need to find a suspect without a name and he may not be local. I have a general physical on him and two identifying marks."

Roy looked worried. "What are those?"

Tenny described the scar and tattoo while Roy made some notes. Then he sat back and shook his head.

"No good news?" Tenny was hoping he might have known some trick to make her search easier.

"Well, we can't search national systems by identifying marks. There is the FBI's violent crime network, but that relies on inconsistent contributions and focuses more on M.O. Do you think this guy has a solid M.O.?"

The thought sickened her. "I hope not."

"Local departments may or may not keep that information on an automated system, but you're talking months for a national search." Roy doodled on his scratch pad as he thought aloud. "You could try the prisons, but that would be making a big assumption."

Tenny finished his thought. "That he had done state time." She looked up and smiled. "We both know how rare that is."

Roy was shaking his head again. "A search of the county jails and prisons would take almost as much time as the local police departments. I think a complete search would be practically impossible."

"Great! The fucker kills, rapes, kidnaps and molests kids, and we can't even find him." Tenny stood and clenched her jaw, not wanting any more misdirected anger to come out.

"Hey, what about state parole?" Roy was still trying to help.

"That's going on the same assumption as state prisons. Plus, their records usually suck." Tenny felt lost in a system of unconnected records. Without a name you had nothing. "Sorry for my little outburst."

Tenny turned to leave as she thought about how unprofessional her behavior had been. As the words replayed in her mind, one stuck — *molest*. That was it!

She practically lunged back at Roy. "He's a molester. He's got to register, right?"

Tenny could tell by the immediate sparkle in Roy's eyes that she had it. "All the states required convicted child molesters to register even if they don't do any time. All the information is in automated systems now. It's a relatively new requirement and some states are just now getting the information automated, but it's there and they can search on identifying marks." Roy stood. "I even have a listing of the telephone numbers for all the systems. They can't be accessed through a national computer system, but you have reduced the work. Let's hope he's been convicted."

He handed Tenny the book with a broad, child-like smile on his face. Tenny thought that he'd make a good detective. He was thorough.

She went over to the Investigative Division and found an empty office. She sat down and got out a pad of paper and pencil. The first call was to Alabama. It was going to be a long day.

The telephone rang several times before somebody finally picked it up. "Hello?"

Great, Tenny thought, I would have to get the girlfriend. But when she spoke Tenny was polite. "Hello, this is Ten . . . Elizabeth Mendoza. May I speak to Carter please."

"She's not feeling well. I don't think you should talk with her. I can give her a message."

"You know that when you tell her that I called she'll just call me back. I need to speak to her about Kelsey."

Blair started into a lecture about what Carter needed when Tenny heard Carter's voice. "Give me the phone."

No argument this time. The phone was relinquished.

"Hi, Carter, it's me. I just wanted to touch base with you. I got back from Portland this morning. I went up there on a long shot which may have paid off."

Tenny went on to explain why she had gone to Portland and what she had discovered. Tenny did not mention who she had found or the details of the extensive crime. Carter didn't need to know the whole truth.

"So anyway, I spent all day today on the telephone and I've narrowed it all down to three suspects. But I want to remind you that this is still a long shot. I doubt that the same man that took Angelica and her sister took Kelsey. But he may be able to lead me to the couple and my gut tells me that they're the answer."

There was a long silence on the other end of the line. Tenny thought that Carter was digesting the information. She had not caught her own mistake.

Finally Carter said, "What do you mean Angelica and her sister? You didn't tell me that it was them, that it was Pearl's girls. You said you went to Portland to see a young girl. What happened to the other one?"

"Shit." She hadn't meant to mention the names.

"Elizabeth, what happened to them? Why did you only speak with one?"

It was Tenny's turn to slide into silence. She closed her eyes, hoping the moment would pass like a bad dream. On the other end of the line, Tenny could feel Carter waiting for the awful truth, already knowing the answer in her heart.

Tenny let the coolness ease throughout her body and answered without emotion, "The youngest is dead."

"Why?"

It would have been easy to pretend ignorance, but she knew that Carter's imagination would create answers as terrible as the truth. She needed the truth. "The suspect in this case had molested the girl and so the couple said

66

she wasn't acceptable. They also said that Angelica wasn't acceptable either because she was too old." Tenny kept that distant, cop tone in her voice.

"What does it mean, not acceptable?"

The fatigue invaded Tenny's professional demeanor. "I don't know, babe. If I knew that I would be much closer to finding Kelsey."

"Tell me what you think. I know you have some ideas."

"I don't. Really I don't have any clue. It could be any one of the things that are always rumored around child abductions. Cult-related, child slavery, illegal adoptions. It could be something none of us have ever dared to dream. I just don't know."

The fear in Carter's voice was more than Tenny could stand. "God, they have my baby. They have my baby!"

It took several minutes to calm her down again. Tenny spoke with confidence and determination about finding Kelsey, which eventually enabled Carter to believe what Tenny herself doubted.

Tenny hung up the phone and was gathering her notes to leave when her old captain walked by the office and glanced inside. His momentum carried him past, but within seconds he was back standing in the doorway.

"What brings you up here to visit and on a day off at that?"

Tenny was cautious. "Just doing a little follow-up on a case."

"Oh really. What case are you working on?" He came in and sat down. Tenny felt trapped.

She avoided his eyes. "It's no big deal. Just something I'm trying not to bother your detectives with."

He stood up immediately, obviously in no mood for games. Tenny knew police work was not to be performed on a personal level. A professional officer could not allow the pain, anger and sorrow to enter into a case. It endangered their objectivity and caused them to over-react. Tenacity had crossed that line.

"Look, Tenny, I know that you spent all day in here making calls to all the fucking states looking for some pervert. Shit, with your reputation you don't think that your peers are going to talk. They're all waiting for you to solve the big one and make that other department look like crap."

He was having difficulty containing his anger. "I talked with your lieutenant. I know what you're doing and I'm telling you it has got to stop." He looked at her, but she felt the determination burning in her eyes. "Damn it, Tenny, we've even gotten complaints from the investigating agency. They claim you're interfering with their investigation."

Tenny raised her voice and cut him off. "I'm not interfering. I'm doing their damn job because they won't do it."

"It's not *your* case. It's not even *our* case and I want you off of it!"

Everybody left in the division was now privy to the shouting match. Tenny rarely raised her voice, but the combination of frustration and anxiety matched her captain's anger.

"This isn't just another fucking case! This is a part of me that has been taken away. You really think I could walk away from that? I'm doing everything on my own time, I'm not asking anything from you or your department."

"It's your department too and if you want to keep it that way then get the fuck off this case. You've crossed the line, Mendoza. Step back now or get out!"

He started to relax as Tenny suddenly grew calm. He seemed confident that she would not jeopardize her career. He eased back somewhat. "I'm sorry it had to come to this, Tenny, but it's for your own good. You can't push this one." He turned to leave.

"Wait, take these with you." When he turned back he was greeted by Tenny's badge and gun which she was shoving into his chest as she walked by. "I quit!"

It felt different driving home. There was a strange sensation of being on the outside. No longer a part of the blue. Yet she didn't feel lost. Instead she finally found herself free from the unrealistic expectations placed on law enforcement officers. Remembering her captain's words, *You've crossed the line*, Tenny announced to the world, "You're damn right I've crossed it and when I'm done there's gonna be a whole lot more people standing on my side of the damn line."

The image of Angelica's strong face and broken hands passed through her mind. Tenny knew that something inside of her had changed forever and somehow her future seemed clear. Finding Kelsey was the first step.

By the time Tenny got home the reality of what she had done was starting to set in. It might have felt right, but what the hell was she supposed to live on — good feelings? Tenny had about eight months' worth of mortgage payments saved and that money wouldn't last long. A month's worth would be used to purchase airline tickets so that she could track down her three suspects. She didn't know anybody in the different jurisdictions where the suspects were. She would not be getting any help.

Oh shit! What authority would she use to obtain the information she needed? She no longer had the badge that had granted her access to anything she needed. What had she done?

Once inside, Tenny went directly to the telephone and

called Ashley. She and her partner, Margo, would have the answers.

Ashley answered the phone, "Hey there."

"What's up gal?"

"Tenny! I'm so glad you called. How are you? How are things going? I'm so sorry for the way we left."

Ashley was talking so fast that Tenny couldn't get a word in and she heard Steve on Ashley's end asking all the same questions.

Tenny yelled over them both, "Hi Steve. Mooching dinner again, huh? How does Margo feel about her adult child?" Halfway through her question, Tenny heard a click on the line and then everybody sounded more distant. "You put me on that damn speakerphone didn't you."

Margo answered, "It's the only way to keep the children from fighting over the phone. Now how are you?"

"Well, I've seen better days and I'm unemployed." Tenny launched into an explanation of the last few days which seemed like a blur even to her. She hadn't realized how fast things had been moving until she relived it for her friends. Tenny finished with the story of the confrontation with her captain.

A long pause and then Steve spoke. "You did the right thing, Tenny. It was time."

Tenny really had no idea what he was talking about, but somehow she knew that Steve was right — it was time.

Ashley immediately began to fill the void which Tenny's resignation would create in the law enforcement environment. Speaking with a command that Tenny had heard only once before in an airport hallway while stalking a killer, Ashley competently issued instructions. "Steve and I will be up there in the morning. Give me the names and last known locations of each suspect and I'll do a little preliminary work tonight. Then in the morning we'll go over what we have and split them up."

"You guys can't do that."

70

Steve sounded confused. "Can't do what? Can't help our friend or can't take the time our department owes us?"

Tenny was insistent. "You can't get involved. This is not your investigation."

Silence and then laughter at the other end of the line. Steve managed to control his amusement long enough to end the conversation. "That was a pathetic attempt. See you in the morning."

The line went dead and Tenny smiled to herself.

Chapter Nine

The doorbell rang. Tenny glanced at the clock in the kitchen. It wasn't even 8:00 AM. Surprised at how early Steve and Ashley actually got there, Tenny went to the front door to greet her friends. The door swung wide but Tenny was not facing her friends.

Carter stood quietly inspecting the ground. Her once fit and sleek body appeared skinny now. The long, trimmed fingernails were bitten down and ragged. When she looked up, her eyes were red and lined with worry.

Little strength was left in her voice. "We need to talk. Can I come in?"

Carter started to move through the entrance, but Tenny didn't move to allow her to pass. She wasn't sure if she wanted to allow this woman inside her house again. How far should she let Carter back into her life? The boundaries had finally been clearly drawn. Now the lines were fading and Tenny was uncomfortable with the uncertainty.

Finally Tenny yielded. "I'm sorry, I was expecting some friends. Please, come in."

Carter entered and walked to the kitchen, where Tenny always spent her time. The living room was for formal occasions. It bothered her that Carter felt comfortable in her home, that Carter knew her habits.

Carter sat at the table while Tenny kept her distance and leaned against a counter. When Carter spoke her pain triggered anger and she sounded like a lecturing parent. "I got a call from Detective Reese. He wanted to know if I had hired you as a private investigator."

Tenny didn't say anything, not knowing how much information Reese had already supplied Carter. Carter immediately read Tenny's expression. "Elizabeth, he told me that he had complained to your department about you conducting a separate investigation into Kelsey's abduction. When the department confronted you, Reese says you quit." Carter searched Tenny's face.

Tenny didn't say anything.

"He said he called me to give you one more chance to back off. He hoped that I could talk some sense into you. He said that if you don't stop your search he'll have you prosecuted for interfering with a police investigation. I don't want you hurt by all this." Carter pleaded despite the tears, "Please, Elizabeth, maybe you should stop. Why are you willing to give up everything for us?"

Tenny was on the verge of tears. "How can you ask that? I'd do anything for you two. I love you guys." Tenny couldn't face her and began to circle the table. "You and Kelsey were my family and I never stopped loving you. I simply learned how to live with my love and without you.

Reese is only trying to save his own butt. He knows he can't put a prosecutable case together against me. So he's using you to get to me. Forget about him."

Carter stood and took Tenny's hands, but neither could look into the other's eyes. Neither could explain why there was still so much love between them, but not enough to bring them back together.

"Carter, after the thing with Pearl, and losing you, I never thought I would be able to piece my life back together again. Everything came apart and I lost the most important things in my life — my confidence, my trust, my sense of right and wrong . . . and you." Tenny pulled Carter close and their cheeks touched. "Now for the first time I feel like I have a chance to put it all together again. It goes much deeper for me than finding Kelsey and I'm not sure I can explain it. But I know in my soul that what I'm doing is the right thing. If I had followed my instincts years ago, none of us would be where we are today. This time I've got to do what's right by nobody's standards but my own."

Carter pulled Tenny away from her cheek and held Tenny's face gently. "You never lost us. We lost you. Tenny, I want . . ."

Carter stopped, stepped back, and tried to control her tears. She touched the tender scar on Tenny's cheek, an injury small by comparison to the scars which this woman bore on her heart. Tenny was searching for so much. They stood there quietly as the love they had for each other filled the room and pushed them further from each other.

Touching Tenny's face one last time Carter began to leave. "Please take care of yourself. I couldn't stand to have something happen to you too." Then Carter saw herself out of Tenny's life once again.

* * * * *

The papers had been discreetly delivered to the hotel in a plain manila envelope. The package appeared to be nothing more than one of the hundreds of business packages the hotel received for its guests every week.

It contained a picture of their future daughter and an explanation of the enclosed forged documents, which were perfect. A visitor's visa in the name of a young niece. The last will and testament of her American parents that granted guardianship to the paying couple. The death certificates for both fictitious parents and the bill of sale for the tombstones that actually marked a final resting place. Everything the couple would need to complete a legal adoption in their own country. It was all so easy. Paper meant so much in the world. If the documents looked real and said it was true, then everybody accepted it as just that — the truth.

The package also included an explanation of what the child should be told. The information referred to several studies by leading child psychologists and reassured them that if the directions provided were followed, then the child would adapt with little or no lasting effects. The child was to be told that it took some time after the doctor rescued her for them to find her mother. Her mother would be joining them soon. They could not wait here, however, because they had to get to a secret place where the bad man who took her couldn't find them.

This way the child would feel safe in her new home. Then, in a few weeks her new parents would explain that her mother and father were killed in an airplane crash on their way to get her. They would comfort the child, love her and give her a new home. There were no other relatives for the child. Nobody else she could turn to for love and support. Her new home would be established and in a relatively short amount of time it would become natural for her.

The last thing the package included were directions to the meeting place where they would receive their new child. The enclosed photograph showed that she was perfect. Exactly what they had requested. Nobody would ever guess that she wasn't born from their genes. They could never have hoped to get such a perfect child from their own country.

It was time for them to leave. They had to get their child and be at the airport in two hours. The United States really was the land of dreams and with enough money, anything could be bought here.

Chapter Ten

"I did a Level Three NCIC computer check on the three names you gave me, Tenny, and got confirmations on all three for last place of arrest or detention. But I still wasn't able to get pictures or decent descriptions of the tattoo or scar. The records people at the arresting agencies couldn't tell me much and I don't think we should rely on the arresting officers either." Steve and Tenny nodded in agreement. Ashley continued, "That means we each get to take a little trip." Ashley handed Tenny and Steve folders. "Steve, yours is relatively close, up in the Sacramento area. His last arrest was in relation to some white supremacist shit, so you be really careful." She turned to Tenny. "Yours hasn't been in trouble for a couple of years. His last place of arrest was outside of D.C., but you might be on a wild-goose chase. I checked several of his arrest records and he always gave the woman listed there on your first page as a person to contact in case of emergencies. She'll probably be the best place to start."

Tenny glanced inside her folder and noticed airline tickets to Washington, D.C., arrest records, and an entire page of information about this woman, including a picture. Glancing up at Ashley, Tenny realized that she was no longer looking at a naïve, ambitious rookie. Instead she was seated across the table from a seasoned investigator and a professional law enforcement officer. For a moment Tenny felt proud, but then she noticed something else.

The innocence was gone from Ashley's face. The sparkle extinguished in her eyes. The quick smile that brightened so many days in the past was rarely seen. Even Ashley's wild, long and free-flowing auburn hair was cut into a short, more professional style.

Several months ago Ashley achieved a position in the Investigative Division as a robbery detective. She was the only woman in the unit and they had immediately loaded her down with the most difficult cases in an effort to prove her incompetent. But the strategy to make her miserable and drive her from their ranks had backfired. Instead, Ashley had plunged into her cases with the persistence and investigative skill she had learned from Tenny. After solving each case with an arrest and conviction, the lieutenant in charge of robbery began to assign her to all the major cases as the lead investigator and Ashley had begun to build a reputation of her own. Yet Tenny knew that this dedication and drive went deeper than professional success. She couldn't help wondering what type of nightmares kept Ashley up at night.

"Tenny, are you paying attention?" Ashley was still speaking and had caught Tenny mentally drifting away from the conversation.

"I'm sorry. I was just thinking." Tenny looked down at her folder. She felt like crying. Steve reached out and took Tenny's hand and gave it a gentle squeeze. Tenny looked into his eyes and Steve gave her a small, knowing smile. How did he always know what she was feeling?

"I know I don't have to, but let me remind you two that we're not acting in any official capacity. Our goal here is not prosecution. Our goal is to find Kelsey. One of these guys is the man who kidnapped Angelica, and he may be the key to finding Kelsey. But if we can find her and still put together some legal evidence and information then that's what we should try to do, so please remember to maintain your professionalism and ethics."

Tenny and Steve both said, "Yes, ma'am," at the same time. Their sarcastic utterance of obedience caused the three of them to stop. As they looked at one another, there was a moment of uncomfortable silence. Nobody knew how to express all the emotions which were being dealt with in that instant.

Finally, Ashley flashed her magical smile and said, "I'm sorry." Suddenly everything was all right again. Seated around Tenny's kitchen table were not three cops, but three friends.

Steve said, "We all know that this goes way beyond the law. We each feel that we are dealing with something big. We're the team to solve this case. We've done big before. We'll find Kelsey."

Tenny had to give her friends one more chance to back out. "You two don't have to do this. I don't want you guys to get into any trouble. Reese is just itching to get somebody fired, especially after I wouldn't give him the satisfaction and quit."

Steve and Ashley were looking at Tenny as if they were confused, as if Tenny had suddenly started to speak some foreign language.

She shook her head. "Thanks."

Tenny checked the map, then checked the street signs at the corner. It should be just two blocks up to her left. She started in that direction. Ashley had given her two full days to complete her investigations in D.C., but she completed her work in less than two hours the day before. She had found the suspect's girlfriend still at the same address that he listed two years ago as he was once again being booked for a petty crime. His girlfriend had politely explained, with little emotion, that he had died about a year ago from a drug overdose. The girlfriend had willingly described his tattoo and Tenny immediately realized that he had not been the right suspect. His death was no loss to her investigation. Tenny wondered if his death had been a loss to anybody.

As she thought about the suspect's death, she came around the corner and found herself staring at the National Peace Officers Memorial. Confronted by the deaths of so many who had meant so much, her chest immediately became tight. Breathing became an effort. For a moment she wanted to keep walking, not willing to draw herself close enough to actually be able to make out the names. But then a marked patrol vehicle drove slowly by and the officer spun the car's emergency lights in a silent tribute to his peers. Tenny knew that she too must thank them.

She started at one end of the low wall which circled toward a shallow fountain. Walking slowly past all the names of officers who had given their lives in the line of duty, Tenny wondered if the nation would ever live peacefully. Each plaque was less than half full with names. There was plenty of room left to add the names of officers who would fall in the future. Too many more would join these officers. Too many more would have to lose their lives in an attempt to protect, in a society where violence was out of control. Tenny couldn't help but wonder if others felt the loss. How many more would it take?

The finger was being jabbed into his face again as the narco agent cursed and threatened. Steve remained unusually calm at such rude behavior but couldn't help momentarily considering snapping that finger from its hand.

"Let me make it perfectly clear to you, Sergeant. This has been a three-year, continuous investigation that has cost big dollars. You are not to interfere in any way. You're out of your jurisdiction and I'll personally make sure you lose your stripes, if not your job, if you so much as drive east when you leave here."

Assistance from the police had not been Steve's first choice, but all his efforts on the streets had yielded nothing. He found that the people at his suspect's recorded places of residence and arrest immediately made Steve as a cop and were unwilling to discuss anything with him.

Apparently, the man he was supposed to track down was a respected member of a white supremacist organization. All of their members and associates knew better than to breathe a word, other than threats, to cops.

Steve had been left with no other options. He had to go to the local cops for information. But they didn't have any information about the tattoo. A booking photo had confirmed the existence of a scar and the booking record mentioned a skull tattoo, but nothing about a snake. He needed to be sure, so he was sent to the Narcotics Division to speak with the agent in charge of a methamphetamine investigation in which his suspect was a part.

Since Steve seemed to have ignored the threats, the agent changed tactics. "I understand that finding this little girl is important. I can imagine how hard .working missing persons must be when it's kids. But this is a crank lab that's turning out enough product each week to supply the whole state. My investigation goes way beyond one little girl. You can understand that, can't you?' You know, the greater good and all that." The agent sat down across from Steve and gave him a big smile, as if they were suddenly the best of friends.

Steve smiled too. "Yeah, I know what you mean. This war on drugs should really take priority. I mean, look at all the good it's doing." His tone turned sarcastic. "Shit, we're really filling those prisons up with some bad characters. Some really dangerous assholes. You know what I mean, don't you." Steve stood and walked toward the door. He stopped and spoke without looking back to the agent. "By the way, she's not missing. She was abducted, just like hundreds of children have been." Then he was gone.

The windows of any vehicle Steve drove were always down no matter what the temperature outside. It was a good habit for any cop. The glass shielded two important senses, hearing and smell, which helped to create the sixth sense that cops prided themselves in having. Yet on this dry dirt road Steve finally yielded to the choking dust and partially cut himself off from the world outside.

The thought that he was making a serious mistake kept encroaching on his concentration. What if that narco cop made good on his threat and called Steve's department? It was one thing for him to take a sudden vacation, but it was something else entirely for him to be jeopardizing another agency's investigation. Steve's job as a cop meant so much to him, nothing else really compared — except for two other cops who had become more than friends. Tenny and Ashley were like family. Tenny needed him and he knew that she would have done the same or more for him without hesitation. Steve snapped his head from side to side, throwing the doubt from his mind.

A dry, hot breeze kept the weightless dust swirling as Steve slowly crept up the road, trying not to divulge his presence with a tail of dust. The inside of the car and Steve already had a thick layer of dirt covering them after traveling two and a half miles up the road from the highway. There were no indications of life along the way. Any adventurer would think this was only a road left to scar the hillside. A reminder of some fool who had gone before and been driven from the valley by the unbearable heat and dust.

Steve wondered how many hidden surveillance cameras he had already passed. If these crooks were as busy as the agent claimed, they wouldn't be taking any chances. He hoped that he looked like an innocent government type, sent on some merciless duty, like to count children, or check zoning, or something. Anything but a nosy cop.

As he crested a small knoll a flash of metal stabbed at his eye. It had come from some shrubbery low to the ground. If they didn't know about his presence before, Steve was sure that they knew now. Still, he continued down the road while picking up his speed. At this point, the appearance of being oblivious to any sinister possibilities became critical.

A large ranch house finally came into view. It was set back into a small group of oak trees which helped to conceal it from overhead surveillance. To the casual observer, the home looked like a great private retreat, with a nice little fence surrounding a well-kept yard and a fresh coat of paint on the house. When Steve saw the house he wanted to turn back.

It was positioned as a fort would be, facing the only road which provided modern attack with vehicles. It sat at the back, the lowest point of a small valley with steep slopes which were filled with large rocks and scattered trees. Instead of having dozens of windows to let in the light and the rustic nature in which the house was situated, there were only a few windows which Steve imagined were heavily fortified.

He kept going and started to remind himself, "You're not a cop. You're not a cop. No cop habits. No cop looks. You're not a cop."

The windshield exploded and shattered but the safety glass refused to shower Steve with deadly shards.

"Shit, you're a fucking cop," Steve shouted as he spun the car to his left trying desperately to keep it on the narrow road while positioning it to give him the most cover possible. He didn't have to guess what had just happened. Some asshole in that fort had warned him to withdraw with a greeting from a high-powered rifle.

As soon as the car came to rest, Steve grabbed his weapon from under his seat and lunged out his door onto the baked dirt, scrambling to safety behind the car's engine block. The car shook as a second bullet ripped through the trunk area. Now they were being so kind as to let him know exactly what he was dealing with, an armor-piercing bullet from a high-powered rifle. Their next shot might not be so polite.

Steve frantically searched the hillside behind him for some cover. Mother Nature still provided the strongest resistance to mankind's destructive weapons. He took five quick breaths, counted to three and sprinted twenty feet up the hill to a large grouping of rocks. He was showered with pieces of granite as he dove for safety. This time he didn't know if it had been a poor shot or just another warning. He really didn't want to find out.

"Shit, now what?" At that moment his pager blasted from his waist, its shrill scream startling Steve more than the fourth shot that pounded into the rocks simultaneously. He grabbed at the pager. It was Ashley with the code they

84

had all agreed on — she had the right suspect in Seattle. "Great, honey, your timing is fucking perfect."

All he had to do now was get the hell out of there. Maybe if he just started to run away, they would let him go. Maybe they wouldn't. He really didn't want to find out. His vehicle was uselessly straddled across the road which provided the only flat surface that wasn't littered with beach-ball-size boulders. It would require several moments of maneuvering to get it into a position for retreat. During that time, he would be an easy target.

Steve's weapon was in his hand, but he was sure he was outnumbered, and his handgun was useless against the rifle. Without back-up officers Steve couldn't risk waiting for darkness. Even then, he was sure the damn gun-of-death that was seeking him was equipped with a night scope.

A sinking feeling invaded Steve's chest. This was worse than the battle in the airport which had almost ended his life. At least then he had help, he had a fighting chance. This time he had not heeded his warnings and had placed his life in jeopardy. Ashley's advice of using caution echoed in his mind as he felt his heart giving up. A voice from his past, a surly training officer from his rookie days, chastised him for a common mistake, *You can't help anybody if you're dead.*

Steve felt a strange vibration in his head. It started as dull, monotone, but grew louder and more intense. Not knowing what was happening to him now, but convinced that it wasn't good, Steve closed his eyes and tried to mentally control the pulsating.

A blast of wind and dust assailed Steve and he snapped his eyes open just in time to catch the "POLICE" written on the belly of the copter as it swooped down at the fortress. Steve jumped up to follow its path and immediately saw the first copter already assaulting the home from the rear, dropping smoke bombs to conceal the path of the second. The second copter did the same to cover the flight of its partner.

Steve was amazed at the perfect execution, but his appreciation was interrupted by the roar of an engine. A huge Chevy Blazer careened backwards down the road which barely accommodated its dimensions.

A back door flung open and Steve caught a quick glimpse of a badge being waved from inside and immediately obeyed the shouted order. "Get the fuck in!"

The Blazer was already accelerating forward when Steve reached the door and flung himself through. The agent looked coolly at him from the front seat. "Thought about your commentary on the drug wars. Figured maybe we can even use you getting yourself killed to nail these guys. Probably should have let them finish you off. Your being alive could screw us in court." The agent smiled. "Get what you were looking for?"

Steve sat up and smiled. "As a matter of fact, I did. But thanks for the help." Steve calmed down, then more to himself than to anybody else who could hear, he exclaimed, "I love the good guys!"

Chapter Eleven

"Where's Ashley?"

Tenny shot the question at Steve without breaking stride or saying hello as she headed from the airline's gate to the curb where she assumed Steve had a car waiting.

Falling into stride, Steve explained, "She's at the prison finishing up the paperwork so that you can interview him."

"How long will it take to drive there?" Tenny glanced at her watch. "Hey, what time is it here anyway?" She had never needed more than a few hours of sleep and the time zones represented nothing more to her than an inconvenience.

"What am I doing?" Steve stopped. "We don't have a

car. We have to fly." Steve looked at his own watch. "Oh shit, we better hustle. The plane leaves in a few minutes. Come on." Steve grabbed her elbow and swung her back around, heading back in the opposite direction.

They walked through the main concourse of the Seattle International Airport and then headed out a smaller one. Eventually they arrived at the gate and Steve quickly checked them in. The attendant led them over to a door, unlocked it and pointed across the pavement at a small plane that was warming up its engines. Steve started toward the plane, but was yanked back by Tenny.

She turned to the attendant, "How many seats are on that?"

"Twelve."

Tenny pulled Steve close and whispered anxiously, "I'm not going on that thing. I hate small planes."

Then turning to the attendant again she informed him, "We'll wait for the next real airplane."

"I'm sorry, miss, but they don't get much larger than this one. The Walla Walla Airport can't accommodate anything larger."

"The what airport?" She looked at Steve. "Where is this guy?"

"He's at the State Penitentiary outside of Walla Walla and it's a six-hour drive from here." He grabbed her and began to walk toward the plane. "Tenny, that plane is how we're going."

Tenny didn't utter one more protest. She climbed into the plane and selected a seat right next to the rear doors. She quickly fastened her seatbelt, grabbed both armrests, leaned her head back against the seat and closed her eyes. She didn't move for the entire fifty-minute flight.

"Come on, Tenny, get in," Steve commanded as he slid

his huge frame behind the steering wheel of the economy rental car.

But Tenny made no move to get in. Instead she began to pace.

Steve leaned over and rolled down the passenger window. "What is it?"

"I don't feel good. Just give me a few minutes to recuperate."

Steve looked more closely at his friend. Her beautiful golden skin appeared a pale yellow, with sweat sticking to it. She was slightly hunched over as she walked with an unsteady, dizzy gait. Steve got out and took a seat on the hood of the car. "What's wrong?"

Tenny looked embarrassed. "I get motion sickness pretty easily. I'm usually all right on real planes, but these little things almost kill me."

Steve couldn't help but smile. So the great Tenacity did have a weakness.

Tenny steered the car into the visitors lot at the prison. Driving with all the windows down had helped to ease her sickness. Plus, she had been planning how she would get the suspect to help her, taking her mind off the queasiness that was still in her stomach.

Ashley walked up to the car as Tenny parked. "You don't look too good."

"She's not feeling well. Seems she has a motion sickness problem and that little plane that got us here wasn't quite her style." Steve jumped out of the car.

"What're you laughing about, Steve? You take pleasure in watching your friend suffer?" Ashley was clearly irritated.

Tenny sensed an argument in the making. "Don't worry about it, Ashley. I'm feeling better and Steve's just scraping together a little confidence for himself because he finally found something he can do better than me." Tenny smiled at him.

He laughed. "You got me there."

Ashley quickly got to the business at hand. "His name's Randy Kouch. He's in his first year of a ten-year sentence for aggravated rape and kidnapping. He has an extensive history for sex-related crimes, including molest, but he's never even been a suspect in any child abductions or murders."

Tenny started toward the gates.

Ashley went on, "Turns out that the same scar and tattoo which Angelica remembered were critical to his identification in the rape case he's here for, which made my job easy." They reached the gates as Ashley finished. "They'll have him in the interview room in twenty minutes, but Steve or I will have to go in with you. They won't allow a civilian to speak with him unless they're family or by his request."

Tenny was annoyed. "Did you explain to them who I am and what I'm doing?"

"And how would you have me explain, Tenny? That you're a great cop that quit her job to chase a hunch and conduct your own personal investigation on a case for which you have no jurisdiction, and which you've been told by the investigating department to stay away from — is that what you wanted me to tell them?"

Tenny was shocked. This was the first time she realized exactly who she was now. Or maybe she finally realized who she wasn't.

Steve took his badge out of his pocket. "Come on, Tenny, I'll go with you."

Tenny noticed a quick flash of disappointment on Ashley's face, but Ashley maintained her stringent professionalism. "That's a good idea. If he won't talk to Tenny, maybe he'll talk to a man."

Steve and Tenny were escorted to an interview room where there was a table with four chairs set around it. Steve lifted one chair and took it to a corner where he had a seat. Tenny seated herself at the table in the chair facing the door which Randy would enter through.

They sat in silence for several minutes before Tenny started to become restless. "What am I going to say to him? Why would he tell me information about crimes for which he's never even been accused?"

"Tenny, don't make a plan. You'll know the right things to say when he's sitting across from you. Trust your instincts," Steve said.

At that moment, the door opened and he was ushered through it with the heavy door snapping shut behind him almost before he was out of its path. He sat down across from Tenny. Tenny slipped once again behind her wall of ice the moment he sat down. The man seated across from her had taken Pearl's life, murdered her grandchild and brought endless pain to Angelica's life. Tenny wanted to beat the shit out of this creature. She wanted revenge. But she needed answers, and therefore none of her hate could surface.

Their eyes locked into a stare that neither would be the first to break. His eyes were a light brown that looked like dirty pennies. One eye remained half closed, forced down by the scar which traveled down through his eyebrow. Tenny could tell he was searching her face for a hint of why she had come. She was careful not to let anything show. Narrowing her stare, she waited for him to ask why she was there. Making him want something first.

She saw the non-verbal signs after just a few minutes. He was beginning to get uneasy. Pushing back from the table somewhat, he attempted to put more distance between them. He would not look away from her but a bead of sweat emerged from his forehead. Tenny needed to increase his discomfort. She needed to communicate to him that he could not hide anything from her. She narrowed her eyes creating a focused beam into his own and soon saw his recognition. She knew everything, the whole deadly truth about him.

"Who are you?" He couldn't disguise the fear in his voice.

Tenny didn't speak. She had to control her anger and vengeance. Those were not the emotions which would get him to talk. His body language already told her that he considered Tenny a threat. This man could not be intimidated into helping. Instead, Tenny was going to have to make him believe that she understood him.

Tenny had always believed that all persons were basically good. It was upbringing, mental illness and society's influence that worked separately or together to introduce evil. She focused on this belief and reminded herself that this man had not been born a murderer and rapist. Maybe somewhere deep inside a piece of good was still present. Tenny would give him a chance to bring it to the surface and help for no other reason than because someone asked.

"My name is Elizabeth. That guy seated in the corner is my friend. He's also a cop. I used to be a cop, but I'm not any longer. We're not here in a formal capacity. I'm looking for a little girl."

He had held her stare until she mentioned the little girl, then his gaze drifted to the top of the table and concentrated on some small detail which only he could see. He said nothing.

"I know about you, Randy." Her use of his name brought only a small flinch. "I know that several years ago you killed a friend of mine and stole her grandchildren. You tried to sell those children to some couple. When they were rejected, you killed one after you raped her. The other child managed to escape, but she never told anybody about what happened until recently."

Tenny was amazed by her calmness. It was if she was making it all up as she went — none of this felt real. Now the hard part.

"I know you had to kill that old woman. She would have fought you to the death for her babies. I'm also sure that killing the child was an accident. But I don't understand why you did it, Randy. What made you take them in the first place? I don't believe that you intended for the children to get hurt. How did you get screwed?"

"Why do you give a damn?" He spoke like a hurt child.

Tenny spoke slowly and was surprised by the lump developing in her throat. "To be honest with you, I don't care. But maybe someday a young woman will come to me and ask me why a stranger took her family and tore it apart, leaving her with nothing. I hope I could tell her something besides . . . because some people are just evil and don't belong among the living."

There was a long pause, then he began to speak, still gazing at the table. "The guy that did that crime probably did it without really knowing the whole story. He was probably a young prick and there was probably a lot of money involved."

Tenny became angry at his denial of his crimes, talking as if he did not know who had committed them. She wanted to interrupt and advise him that if she wanted to charge him with murder, she could without his confession. Christ, she had an eyewitness. The cop in her was begging to pound the table and announce to this shithead that he would be spending the rest of his life in prison. Yet that was not what had brought her here. His prosecution would not stop the abductions and the deaths. True justice could not be served by revenge. This man was responsible for single, horrible acts, but his punishment would not create good. Justice needed to start constructing a model for change and not simply control the spread of evil.

Kelsey was still out there and he was her only hope. Tenny sat quietly and buried her anger as he continued. "He probably didn't have too much respect for life. Probably spent his whole fucking life fighting for his own shitty existence, always wondering why he even bothered." He stopped.

Tenny shook her head. "Such a delicate balance between good and bad. Such a thin line between hope and hopelessness."

He raised his head and looked at her. "How come you ain't judging me?"

"I'm not a judge. I'm only trying to find a little girl and I need your help." Tenny could tell that she had gotten through to him.

He sat forward. "I heard about the job on the street. The word was out that somebody was looking to buy this kid. They wanted a little black girl. Shit, they had a mess of rules about how the kid was supposed to be, but I didn't pay attention to those. I figured any black girl would do and I had just seen these two homeless kids. Shit, I convinced myself that I would be doing them a favor. I called the number I had and somebody gave me a meeting place. It was going well, but then that asshole woman said that I had fucked the little girl and she wouldn't take her. Then they just left me with those two kids. What the fuck was I supposed to do? I didn't mean to kill the little one, I was just working off some steam."

Tenny couldn't take it anymore. He hadn't even mentioned Pearl. He made it sound as if it was everybody else's fault. There was no sorrow for anybody but himself. Tenny had to get out of here, but she needed more. "Tell me about the woman. She's still buying children, and she's still probably fucking up people's lives like she did with yours."

"The bitch was a snooty, upper-class cunt. Prancing around that room giving orders like she was some type of fucking queen. Lecturing me about how she would have me thrown in jail if I ever said anything about her to anybody else."

He laughed and threw up his arms. "Well, here the fuck I am anyway. But there's nothing to tell. I don't know who the fuck she was. Just that she was a bitch and had funny eyes."

Tenny heard something in the corner. She had forgotten Steve was there, but now he was sitting forward in his chair. They both wanted an answer to the next question.

Tenny asked, "What do you mean by funny eyes?"

"Oh, they were weird. Fuck, one was brown and one was blue. Shit, she probably wasn't even human."

He went on ranting about the she-devil, but Tenny no longer heard a word he was saying. She remembered a woman with one blue and one brown eye leaning over her, offering to help. The woman had said she was a doctor. Tenny bolted from her chair and rang the bell on the wall. Steve was beside her as the guard opened the door.

Tenny burst through the door and began to jog through the corridors leading to the outside, frustrated by the slow, cautious procedures for allowing anybody outside the walls of this prison. She remembered the woman doctor who had come to her aid at the bicycle crash. Kelsey had disappeared the next day. Tenny exploded through the final gate and sprinted to the car where Ashley was waiting. Finally, she had them!

BOOK TWO

Chapter Twelve

The coffee house was bustling with night people loading up on caffeine to help them through the late hours. Tenny sat at a small table against the back wall and sipped from her second *café au lait*. The adrenaline rush had worn off during the trip from Seattle back to Bayview. The fifteen hours, most of which were spent in a car or on an airplane, were starting to dull her mind. But the chemical reaction generated in her body by the coffee had Tenny growing antsy as she waited for Frederick. Checking her watch again, it was now one minute after ten and he was late.

Frederick and Tenny had started together in the academy, both determined to get on the fast-track to success. Their competitiveness had eventually evolved to admiration and friendship. Their paths in the department had gone in different directions, but they had always relied upon each other when it counted. In fact it had been Frederick who was there in the end when she had finally captured Whittington.

A week ago, when Tenny quit, Frederick had been furious. His anger had been so intense that they had not spoken since that time, that is until today. Earlier this afternoon, Frederick had listened carefully as Tenny described her discoveries and he had immediately agreed to meet her with the copy of her accident report, but he probably intended to give her a huge dose of reality when he saw her.

As he entered the coffee house, Tenny immediately focused on the folder which Frederick was carrying with him. It took all of her self-control not to rush him and strip it from his hand. Instead, Tenny glanced one last time at her watch — 10:03 PM.

"You're late."

Frederick glanced at his own watch and smiled. "You're right. We agreed to ten, didn't we." He sat and placed the folder on the table with both elbows firmly on it.

"Where's my mocha?" But as he spoke the young girl that had been busily creating coffee stimulators appeared at his side and placed a mocha down in front of him.

Tenny smiled at her. "Thank you."

"Some things never change. You still take care of me, don't you, Tenny?" Frederick relaxed and took a sip of his drink.

"Just as you do me. Now may I see the report, please?" Tenny reached for the folder.

Slipping the folder to his lap, Frederick became serious. "Not so fast. We have some things to talk about first." Tenny knew a lecture was coming. "Do you really know what you're doing? Shit, you quit your job. You continue to pry in an investigation which you've been warned to stay out of, and now you want to pursue a hunch."

"I know it's them." Tenny was defensive.

"How could you know? You're basing an assumption on nothing more than coincidences." Frederick was becoming angry. "You got lucky and found Angelica, now you want to stretch a small piece of information she gave you into a theory. We both know that's not how it works."

Tenny tried to explain her intuition. "Look, we also both know that solving cases is like putting a puzzle together. I've gotten lucky, when I dumped the pieces out, a bunch of pieces were already stuck together. All I need to do is fill in the gaps." Tenny stuck out her hand. "Those names you have will fill in a big missing piece."

"How do you know?" He seemed frustrated. "All you have is a woman doctor with different-color eyes in the area at the time Kelsey disappeared."

"Don't forget the rest of Randy's description. He described her to a tee." Tenny remained calm, although she wanted to jump him and rip the damn folder from his grasp. "It's more than a hunch. I know that it's them."

"Fine, say you're right. Say it is this couple. My question remains the same. Do you know what you're doing?"

Losing her patience, Tenny coolly replied, "I've been right in the past and I've always been able to handle what I started."

Frederick leaned forward and hissed, "This is different! Damn it Tenny, I've done some checking on these people and you're out of your league. We're not talking about some street punk criminals that kill while committing another crime. We're not talking about murders induced by passion. We're not even talking about a damn serial rapist that acts out of some perverse understanding of the world. These people you're after don't make mistakes!"

He sat back and took another sip of his mocha, trying

to calm down. "Look, you and I both know that they're not offering to buy children so that they can molest them or kill them. This whole sick thing is about money. There's nothing more dangerous than money."

They sat there staring at each other. He was right, but she couldn't stop now. "May I see that folder please?" This time Frederick relinquished it.

Tenny immediately searched for the names as he filled her in, "They live in Chicago. He's an international attorney of some sort and she's a doctor. They are one of Chicago's favorite couples and they've never had any run-ins with the law. In fact, they donate to some of law enforcement's causes. There are going to be many unhappy people if you start prying around in their lives."

Tenny looked up from the folder, her eyes burning. "They're stealing kids and selling them for God knows what. I don't care how many unhappy assholes there are."

"Please, Tenny, I trust you and your hunches, but please be careful. I've got a really bad feeling about this one."

Tenny touched his hand and smiled. "I'm always careful."

Be careful! The words kept pounding their warning in her mind as she headed home. Tenny was never the type of cop to let her ego control her actions. Maybe she *was* in over her head. Maybe she *did* need help. If so, she needed somebody with authority. Steve and Ashley were already back in Los Palos and they had helped enough.

Going directly to the phone when she arrived home, she dialed Betsy's number. It was time for the truth.

The phone rang only once and then its angry ring was

silenced and Betsy's weary voice answered, "This better be good."

"It's me and you can skip the coffee this time. I don't think you'll need it."

"What's wrong?"

"Don't you bullshit me anymore! You didn't think I would get this far did you?"

"Tenny, I —"

"You didn't, did you!" Tenny was on the verge of yelling. "Look, I know that you didn't get fired because you fuck women. And when you said 'battle' last time, that's what you meant, wasn't it? It's a battle you lost, didn't you? You were working them when you found Angelica, weren't you? You've known about them for years, haven't you? Damn it, haven't you?" Tenny was going so fast Betsy didn't have time to say anything. Tenny fought back the tears. "I want the truth from you, Betsy. I need it!"

"Okay, honey, it's okay. Please don't be angry. I just didn't want you to get hurt. You're right, I should have known that you would find them." Betsy sighed. "Tenacity."

"Stop trying to protect me. I'm not a brand new rookie anymore. I'm not new at anything." Tenny was pleading, "Talk to me, tell me what you know."

"I don't know where to start." Betsy paused, but Tenny said nothing. "Several years ago I got impatient with the research that was being done into child abductions, so I did some of my own. I listed out all the locations of abductions for the last five years. Then I went to the closest major metropolitan area and checked the newspapers for the week before and after each abduction. I didn't know what I was looking for at first, I was just fishing for anything out of the ordinary which I could turn into a pattern."

"I did sort of the same thing, but I didn't find anything." Tenny was regaining her composure.

Betsy sounded like she was still on edge. "Well, I discovered something definitely out of the ordinary. In each abduction except for two there was a coin show in the nearby city. Plus, in the other two cases, there was a coin show within one hundred miles."

"A coin show?"

"Somebody was dealing in more than coins." Betsy was becoming excited again as she went on. "The problem was that these shows attract coin collectors, hobbyists and nerds from all over. There was no way to narrow it down without some more information about the suspect or suspects."

"That's why you were so quick to answer my message and arrive when Pearl's children were taken." Tenny was beginning to understand. "You were already here. Was there a coin show?"

"Yes."

"So the Feds knew somebody was going to get snatched. What the hell did you do to stop it?"

"Nothing, damn it! It was still only my hunch and there had already been several shows where nothing happened." Betsy sounded as if she was fighting not to lose her own composure. "The administration had just about decided that I was off track and was getting ready to pull the plug on my investigation."

"But after Pearl they didn't need any more convincing." Tenny knew how the politics worked.

"Well, they weren't convinced, but they were willing to let me work it some more. But I couldn't stand letting another child get snatched when we were so close. I couldn't think of a way to catch them, but I could stop them." Betsy paused as if she was momentarily confused. "Or at least I thought I could."

"How could you stop them? What could you do?"

"Well, I dragged a bunch of hotshot agents with me and we started hitting cities that were hosting coin shows about a month before the show arrived. You're not talking about that many shows a year so the Agency bought off on sending us in to do an ounce of prevention. We provided extra training to local law enforcement, hosted meetings with school PTAs, and we even went out on the streets to identify street children and at least attempt to talk to them. We wanted to make sure —"

"That's how you found Angelica," Tenny interrupted.

"Yes, but she wouldn't talk to me about what happened. Not a word, no matter what I said or did." Betsy waited, as if hoping that Tenny had heard enough.

"Well, what happened?" Tenny was not satisfied.

"What do you mean?"

"Betsy, I know the story doesn't end there."

Betsy laughed sarcastically. "Well, now you're wrong. It does end right there. There were no more abductions for a while probably because they found out about our efforts. They stopped and I gave up."

"You don't give up." Tenny knew better. "Tell me about the Jenkinses."

"You really are good. Yeah, that's them, Chicago's favorite citizens. You can't mess with them, Elizabeth."

"Tell me, Betsy. Who the hell are these people?"

"I've told you enough already." Betsy was silent. But the quiet tomb between them was not filled by Tenny, and Betsy couldn't take it after a few moments. "Angelica did make a slip about 'the doctor' once when she was angry about having to get a medical in order to attend that private school. I just kind of ran with that because I had nothing else. But as soon as I took a look at the Jenkinses I got into trouble. I was asked to back off and I didn't. Then I was asked to resign."

Her anger was resurfacing. "What? Are you telling me that the fucking FBI was bought by them? You were doing your job!"

Betsy's own rage burst from her. "What I was doing was trying to prove a case without any hard evidence. I had nothing and I was picking on the wrong people. What do you have? No, you don't have to answer, I already know — you have nothing!"

Tenny felt lost and confused. Betsy had always been her idol. "I don't understand how you could just give up. Betsy, we're talking about children. They're taking children. You used to care so much. The passion you had when you talked about crimes against children was hypnotizing. It was addictive and you touched me. I thought we shared that. How could you give up?"

Tenny was sorry she had said it the moment she had finished. As she listened to her friend weep on the other end of the line, Tenny knew that Betsy's passion had consumed her these past few years and left her empty.

Finally after minutes of tears, Betsy said, "I didn't change. I was beaten. They played the game better than me. When I realized I couldn't win, that I couldn't stop them, I had to get out. I couldn't face my failure. I just wanted to forget." More silence, then Betsy whispered, "I'm telling you, you won't win either. I had the support of the federal government and couldn't prove a thing. The Jenkinses made me look like a fool. They destroyed my reputation and my career. If I hadn't backed off, I guarantee you, they would have destroyed me! You won't win!"

"Yes, I will. I quit my job." Tenny spoke with calm determination, drained of all other emotions. "I'm not in this to prove a case. I'm just looking for a little girl and I won't stop until I find her." Tenny hesitated. "Now I need your help. I need somebody in Chicago with some authority who will help. You must know somebody."

106

The long pause revealed Betsy's shock that Tenny had given up her job, her security and her future in preparation for the battle. Betsy still had one thing she too could offer. "Her name's Caroline, but they call her Skates. She takes the most difficult cases and just glides right through them, hence the nickname. She's a Deputy District Attorney in the Windy City. She also happens to be considered one of the experts in the nation on crimes against children. She's the best, even better than you."

Chapter Thirteen

Joao Sousa knew that such a special child could not have been the result of money alone. She was meant to be their daughter and to carry on his family, if not its name. He watched his wife, Carlota, and the beautiful child read quietly on the porch and was proud of how quickly she was learning their native language. Kelsey was smart, energetic, with the same spark of imagination and determination which had brought his family to its treasured standing in his country. His great-great-grandfather would have approved of this child. Though she didn't have their blood, she did have their spirit.

His great-great-grandfather had founded their mining

business in this small mountain town. It was also here that he had built their family home which had been passed down along with the business. Each generation of boys had become men, and with their maturation they each had expanded the business. It had been Joao's father who had finally moved their offices from this small town, fast becoming a historical site, when he was no longer able to accommodate the pace of the family's growing mining business. But their home had remained, and he made the two-hour commute twice a week into the new state capital where he kept an apartment for his weekday nights.

The family fortune had increased; he was the chairman of an international mining corporation. He smiled. Not bad for a poor family that immigrated to this country with nothing. The United States was not the only country of opportunity.

Yet the spiritual leader of the tribal gods had warned his great-great-grandfather that with happiness must come pain and sorrow. His family's curse was the most hurtful thing that could have been bestowed on such a grand progeny — the inability to continue.

His great-great-grandfather had only been able to have one child, a son. His great-grandfather had grown to be a fine man who brought many riches to his family and the town. But the curse prevented his great-grandfather from giving the same strength and stability to the family that he gave to the community. A single son was all that his great-grandmother could bear.

His grandfather had challenged the hex and brought both a boy and a baby girl to the family. Years later the daughter had died in childbirth and her infant had perished days later, once again leaving only a son. His own father had been blessed by the birth of three sons, only to lose the two oldest in a terrible mining accident. Joao had been forbidden to enter the mines after that accident, which had helped to make him a formidable businessman. But it had not stopped the curse, which had come to life in his blood, creating sterility.

His best friend, an attorney for his corporation, had mentioned an international adoption opportunity. The Sousas had already explored adoption in their own country and were disappointed. Therefore he was anxious to learn about international opportunities. When he discovered that it was a black market operation he hesitated, but the assurance that he could have the exact child that he wanted convinced him to participate.

The request for a little girl had been for his wife. At this point in their family history, sex didn't matter. His family would bear no more children, but with Kelsey it would live. It was time to tell her.

"Kelsey, my little one, come in here."

She sprang from Carlota's lap and came dancing in from the porch. Her movements were so magical and free that they created their own music which he too could hear.

"Come here to my lap."

Kelsey smiled as if she still found his awkward English amusing. His wife had studied languages for years and her English was almost fluent, so Kelsey only got to gently tease him. He loved her polite corrections and playful mimicking.

"There is news of your mother and father." The excitement which shot through her body and emanated from her eyes almost broke his heart. Carlota, who knew what was coming, turned her back. He took her small hand tightly in his own and as he looked into her deep brown eyes, his tears began. The sorrow for what he was about to do weighed on him. He bowed his head in silence. He knew that he had to end one family. It was the only way to save his own. "Your parents have died in an aircraft accident. They were on their way here for you."

The body of his little dancer stiffened on his lap. Her grasp on his hand tightened as her eyes widened and became unfocused with a terror he could not see or imagine. He did not hear the breath escape from her, but her breathing had stopped. Before his eyes, a child was dying.

Kelsey was confused. It didn't make any sense. She could not understand any of the events which had taken place over the past month. If these people knew her parents, then why hadn't she talked to her mother? There was a phone in all the places she had been. Why hadn't they let her talk to her mom, before it was too late. Now it was too late!

Kelsey felt the arms around her hugging her tighter and could feel his love. Being here was not scary. It was like being at home in a way. The only thing missing was her mom.

Burrowing her face against his neck, Kelsey felt the tears begin. She didn't know what it meant. What would happen now if her parents were gone? Without her mother, who would stay beside her at night when she was frightened? Kelsey understood death; her mommy was gone and wasn't coming back. But what she didn't comprehend was what death meant to the living. Before when somebody had died, they had just gone on with life after saying good-bye. The *they* had been her mother and herself. Now, there was no way to go on. She was alone.

"My little one, you will stay here. We will make our home yours. We will help you to grow in a way to make your parents proud as they watch from above." He held her tight and let her exhaust her tears. Then he pulled her tenderly away from him and let her new mother hold her. "You will not be alone," he assured her.

Kelsey touched the birthmark on her neck. "Will Elizabeth be coming for me now?"

She saw a strange expression spread quickly across his face as he looked to his wife. "Darling, we were told by the American authorities that you had no other family. Who is this Elizabeth?"

"She's my friend. I'll stay here until she comes for me."

He gently pried for more information. "Where can we contact her so that she may come?"

Kelsey did not understand the question. She slowly shook her head. "No, she's a police officer. She will come for me. My mommy told me that Elizabeth would come for me if anything ever happened to her."

Slowly the horror returned to Kelsey's eyes as reality settled into her young mind. She started to beg for this woman that they knew nothing about. Finally came sobs as Kelsey began to face a tomorrow without her mother and father.

His tears would not stop either; his family was threatened once again.

Chapter Fourteen

After ending her conversation with Betsy, Tenny had made arrangements to fly to Chicago. The next morning, she called Carter to give her a brief update. She tried to balance the news with hope and doubt. The last thing Carter needed was the rollercoaster of emotion between anticipation and disappointment.

Next Tenny caught Ashley as she arrived at the office. Tenny gave her the information she had from Frederick and told her about Caroline VanDere. She had to make sure to cover all her bases. She didn't know what to expect in Chicago.

A few hours later, sitting in the waiting area of the District Attorney's offices, Tenny wondered how much

Betsy had told this Skates woman. What made Betsy think this woman would risk her career on a case which had destroyed two already? How could Tenny be sure that she wouldn't simply sabotage her efforts, while protecting two of Chicago's favorite residents? Shit, what made Tenny think she could march right into enemy territory and find allies? She stood to leave. She would continue her search alone.

"Miss Mendoza, Miss VanDere will see you now. It's the third office on the right." The secretary interrupted her escape.

Tenny expected to find a striking woman, someone matching the impressive reputation Betsy had attributed to Assistant District Attorney VanDere. Instead, seated behind the desk was a small woman, sturdy in build. Trim eyeglasses were sliding to the tip of her nose, and set off the roundness of her face as she studied some paperwork on the desk in front of her. Red hair highlighted the freckles scattered over her face. If it hadn't been for the severe manner in which she had done her hair and her manicured appearance, VanDere could easily have been mistaken for a teenager.

Tenny wondered what made this woman so imposing to others. Then VanDere spoke. "Stop trying to figure me out with one look. Get in here, shut the door, and have a seat, Ms. Mendoza." Her voice carried the autocratic background which her name implied. Tenny yielded to its innate authority.

She attempted to be polite. "You can call me Tenny."

"Oh, you mean the great Detective Tenacity. Well Betsy and I had a long conversation this morning and as I understand it you are simply Ms. Mendoza again. In fact, the investigating agency seems to think you're interfering in their investigation. Your tenacity has taken you too far this time. So far the *investigation* you have performed has yielded you nothing that can be used in a court of law.

114

You've based your suspicion on coins and the color of a woman's eyes." VanDere's voice grew colder. "Worse than that, your sloppy tactics and unprofessional approach have left us with useless information which I can't even redeem in any way. All we have is a miserable teenager who can identify a killer, but not the scum who hired him." She pushed back from her desk. "And as far as I can see you have that prick in prison who's toying with you. Sure, he may have got you here, but he'll never testify and the best offer that any prosecutor could make would be life. He's due to be released in six years." VanDere clamped her fingers around her pencil, as if she was about to throw it at Tenny. "Shit, we can't even use his admission to you because there was a damn cop in the room." She shook her head. "What the hell were you thinking? Ms. Mendoza, you have allowed your emotions to interfere with your use of good judgment."

Tenny did not let her gaze stray from the D.A.'s penetrating gray eyes. She sat quietly as VanDere stood and rounded the desk. Her finger came up in a denunciatory manner and was jammed in Tenny's direction.

"You're accusing one of Chicago's favorite couples of child abduction. Are you nuts? He's an international attorney that has assisted our fucking president at times. She's a leading pediatrician. Did you hear what I said? A pediatrician! She saves children!"

VanDere was standing over Tenny with her finger jabbing at Tenny's chest. No one stuck their finger in her face. The cop in Tenny was alive and well. But Tenny controlled her anger and stood up without ever letting her eyes stray from VanDere's. Once she was standing, Tenny slowly let her gaze drift from VanDere's face to her finger which was still pointing in Tenny's direction. VanDere quickly withdrew it.

Tenny stared at the D.A. Her anger made her voice turn to the icy coolness that had always made everybody around her back off, no matter what the situation. "I'm sorry to have wasted your time, Ms. VanDere. There must have been some sort of mistake. I was told that you were good. Obviously, you're intimidated by the case which faces you now. Either that, or you're too blind to realize that this man and this woman are the most dangerous criminals that we have in our society. They're accepted as good people for *what* they are, not *who* they are." Tenny walked to the door. "Thank you for sharing your opinions so I didn't waste any more of my time with you — Skates." Then she was gone.

Unwilling to spend one more unnecessary second in the building, Tenny didn't even wait for the elevator. She vaulted down the stairs, using the hand railings to propel her over entire sets of steps, her anger releasing itself each time she pounded to the bottom of a flight. As she burst through the door on the ground floor, she almost collided with VanDere. She was waiting in the lobby.

VanDere grabbed Tenny's arm and started to drag her toward the ladies' room. Tenny tried to rip free of VanDere's grasp but couldn't. She had a firm hold of Tenny's jacket. More force would be necessary to disengage herself from this spineless imitation of a champion for children. Tenny elected to wait until she was freed voluntarily, then she would simply walk away. Any other physical attempt by VanDere to detain her would meet with a painful example of the police skills she still had.

When they entered the ladies' room, VanDere used an invisible strength to whip Tenny past her and released her grip. Yet she blocked Tenny's access to the door. Betsy had obviously warned her about Tenny.

Before Tenny could threaten bodily harm, Caroline spoke. The authority was gone from her voice. In its place was an angry confusion that deepened her tone. "You didn't let me finish. I've worked for fifteen years doing nothing but my damn best to protect children. That whole

116

time these people have been right under my fucking nose, destroying children and families. I'm going to nail them for everything, including homicide. I'm after *them*. You're after *one* child. They're your only chance to find her, but you have to back off and let me work this case. There are more children out there waiting to become victims. Let *me* save them."

Tenny took a deep breath and fought back tears. "Kelsey is still alive."

"I hope you're right. But you have to slow down. We can't sacrifice all the others to save her. If they get tipped that we're this close, they'll cover up anything that we might be able to use, but they won't stop. We both know that they won't be frightened enough to run. We need a legal case against these monsters. An airtight case which will stop this madness." Caroline reached out and took Tenny's hand. "Please trust me. Let me help. If we get our case against them, then we'll find Kelsey."

Tenny took her hand away. "What are you going to do?"

"I'm going to start with a friend of mine who works for the IRS. Taxes have landed many big fish, especially in this town."

"I'll give you two weeks and then we'll see where we are. Meanwhile I'll do a little research." Tenny began to step around Caroline.

"Not so fast, Tenacity." Caroline stepped in front of her but made no effort to touch her. "You're going to stay with me while you're in town so I can keep an eye on you. Meet me in front in five minutes. I drive a blue Ford Explorer."

"This is a Frank Lloyd Wright home." Tenny could hear the admiration in her own voice.

"That's right." Caroline seemed surprised. "How did you know that?"

"Oh well, residential architecture is kind of a hobby for me." Tenny tried to conceal the excitement she was feeling about actually getting inside one of his homes.

"Well, it's really no big deal. I managed to keep the house in the divorce, even though it was my husband's treasure. He shouldn't have married an attorney." Caroline pushed open the front door. "It's a little stiff and bare. My husband, I mean my ex-husband, wanted to keep it as close to Wright's vision as possible. I haven't bothered to liven it up yet."

Tenny set her bag down and walked out into the living room. She stood perfectly still in the center and turned slowly, looking at the room from ceiling to floor. There was a row of windows at shoulder level which ran around the entire room, which was elevated from street level. The windows gave the impression of being much larger because of the amount of scenery and light which they brought to the room. To create even more of a feeling of openness in a room with a low ceiling, Wright had fitted etched glass into the interior doors opening to the room, helping to maximize the space. Tenny thought it was so like Wright to try and get everything he possibly could out of each project — nothing ever wasted.

"It's beautiful, so sharp, so clean, so fitted. Everything takes advantage of everything else. His vision was truly whole. He saw so much more than everybody else." Tenny felt like she was in a trance. "May I look around?"

"Go ahead. Just pick an empty room and make it yours. I apologize for the furniture, it's all his stuff too. It fits this place, but it's not the most comfortable stuff in the world." Caroline started out of the room. "I'll be in the kitchen."

Tenny crept up the stairs and went into the first room at the top. She was studying the ceiling trim as she walked into the room and she bumped into some type of table set in the middle of the room. Tenny glanced down, slightly annoyed that somebody would set furniture in the middle of a room.

"Oh shit!"

The Dane stood inches from her and its head came up to her chest. Its black coat shone with the wealth of black gold. Its teeth were tremendous, lethal-looking. It was slim, but its body was cut into the form of a champion. For a moment Tenny relaxed as the beast looked to the door. Maybe it would just leave.

The animal leapt at Tenny and put a front paw on each of her shoulders. Now Tenny was looking up to its head, which towered above her own.

Caroline laughed as she stepped into the room. "Moose, get down." Moose gave Caroline a confused look and obeyed. Caroline couldn't stop laughing.

"My God, that's a horse." Tenny felt safe with Caroline in the room and couldn't help smiling as Caroline hugged her Moose who also seemed to be laughing at her.

"Don't worry. She's harmless. In fact, she's quite happy to have a guest. It's another person to pay attention to her. Moose is sure that she is a deprived Dane."

Tenny reached out and stroked Moose's head.

Caroline had one last burst of laughter. "You two can settle in and then come downstairs."

Moose watched her owner leave the room and then looked up again at Tenny, considering whether to stay with the immediate gratification of the petter or follow her provider. After a moment, Moose padded off down the stairs after Caroline. Tenny quickly unpacked, then followed.

"Can I help with anything?"

"No thank you." Caroline smiled. "I'm only making something simple. I thought I would grill a little chicken with some vegetables in a honey-mustard sauce. Then I opened some wine and thought maybe it would be good in the sauce. Then I thought that this probably wouldn't be enough, so I decided to put it over a bed of pasta. Regular egg fettucini sounded boring, but I found some squash pasta and a little spinach pasta so I just combined them. Everything should be ready in a minute or so. Do you want a glass of wine?"

Tenny smiled and nodded yes. She couldn't speak. Caroline had taken her breath away. While Caroline was talking about cooking, her eyes had glistened with enthusiasm. Her speech had become light and quick with excitement. Her smile had been easy and often. But most of all, her comfortable laughter had rung with a freedom which created something similar to magic. Assistant District Attorney VanDere was no longer average in her appearance, she was stunning.

Caroline began to blush when she handed Tenny a glass of wine and noticed her admiration. She turned back to the stove. "So I'm actually kind of a fan of yours."

"Oh really?" Tenny found it hard to believe after the berating she had received.

"Yeah. I saw the television special about your rape investigation. I was very touched by it." Caroline faced her again.

"Then you're a fan of Diane Barker. It was her program." Compliments made Tenny uncomfortable.

Caroline was direct. "No, I think you were the key to the whole investigation. You held your team together. You got the community together. Besides, you're the one that finally caught that bastard."

It was Tenny's turn to look away. "Well, I wish you would give me that much credit now."

The comment made Caroline pause. "I guess I did come off a little hard earlier." Caroline appeared to be at a loss for words. "It's just ... it means so much to me to stop them."

Tenny was looking Caroline in the eyes. "Not nearly as much as it means to me."

Chapter Fifteen

"Here's my work number and my pager number." Caroline was standing at the front door as Tenny leaned against the wall sipping her coffee. "There's a little store about three blocks down if you need anything I don't already have." Caroline pointed over her shoulder in the direction of the store. "I'll call and check in with you later this morning."

Tenny smiled. "Don't bother, Mom. I won't be here." Moose wandered into the hall, saw the look of displeasure on Caroline's face, and decided that Tenny would be her best bet for a little head rub.

"What exactly do you plan to do today?" It wasn't a friendly inquiry.

Tenny scratched Moose's head. "I thought I'd do a little work. Don't worry, I won't screw things up anymore." Her tone was sarcastic.

"Look, I already apologized for yesterday." Caroline glanced at her watch. "You've actually gotten really far with your hunches. But now it's time to let me wrap things up in a nice tight prosecution package. That's why you found me, right? So that I could help?" Tenny looked away. "Just stay out of trouble, all right?" Caroline opened the door. "Moose would love you forever if you took her for a walk." Then she was gone.

Moose looked longingly up at Tenny.

The building looked more like a warehouse, rust brown with green pillars and large ventilation vents gusting out used air. Tenny walked around the whole building, which occupied an entire block, before she found the entrance that had the classic Gothic ornamentation. Inside, there was no mistaking what this building housed — knowledge. Tenny found a directory for the library and headed toward the periodicals room. The room was full of computers and viewers, everything state-of-the-art equipment. Tenny knew her way around libraries, even the best, and went and sat down at an empty terminal.

Hours of rummaging through the *Chicago Tribune* and smaller local newspapers revealed much about the public lives of the Jenkinses. He specialized in international trade agreements and was thought to be one of the nation's experts. He had served on several special committees for his country, capturing the attention of the White House. There were even articles about rumors of a Cabinet position a few years ago.

It also turned out that Tom Jenkins and his wife were extremely charitable, often the hosts of extravagant fundraisers for a variety of causes. Tenny printed an article which pictured them with their son, who had just been accepted to college in premed. They were co-hosting a dinner to raise money for the National Center for Missing and Exploited Children.

As Tenny gathered her things, the audacity stabbed at her. The tears rushed to her eyes as she hurried from the library. Today she had put together more of the pieces and they were constructing a formidable wall between her and Kelsey.

Walk, walk, walk. Tenny needed to think. She forced the tears back. She reminded herself that everybody could be brought down in some way. She had gotten this far. The prestige, the connections, the wealth — none of these would stop her. Tenny finally realized why Betsy had been forced to give up, defeated in the pursuit of justice. She also understood the warnings from Betsy, Frederick and Caroline. They had appreciated the complexity of her task, but they did not understand her motivation. Tenny wasn't pursuing society's prescribed justice. She was after so much more, a correction of a wrong and not simply a punishment for the guilty. Even more, she was searching for the confidence to rely on herself and her belief in what was right.

The nature of the crime was simple for Tenny to comprehend. Children were being taken and sold. But what was their value? She considered the price of a child. What did it cost to tamper with the future? Tenny wondered why a legitimately wealthy couple would risk everything. Yet Tenny knew the answer. It was part of this culture that nobody ever had *enough* of anything. The great American motto — MORE!

She stopped and took a deep breath. She found herself

facing a park. She started into it and as she reached the crest of a small hill, she saw the water. It looked like the ocean and drew her toward it. There was something unusual about the water. Normally it settled her. Today its quiescence made her tense. Suddenly the water became sinister.

It became clear to her. Tom Jenkins, the international attorney, dealt in the commodity of children. It was perfect. Outside the boundaries of United States law enforcement, the children were hidden in their new families. The Jenkinses thought that the children were beyond reach. They were wrong.

Chapter Sixteen

"Moose and I are ready." Caroline came lightly into the kitchen, where Tenny was huddled over a cup of coffee. She glanced at Caroline, who was dressed in jeans, a sweatshirt and street hikers.

"Those don't look like work clothes."

"Took the day off." Caroline turned off the coffee maker. "I thought it was time to get you out of the house, away from those damn articles that you've read a hundred times, and show you Chicago. Come on, we should have something from the IRS tomorrow. Sitting around here won't make it come any faster." Caroline tugged her up by the arm.

"Are you pushing me around again, Counselor?" Tenny tried to sound annoyed.

"Absolutely! Chicago's not all bad and I'm going to prove it to you beyond a reasonable doubt."

As Caroline pushed her toward the front door, Tenny complained, "God, I hate high energy people."

Caroline leashed Moose and put the strap in Tenny's hand. There was no turning back. Moose had a big day ahead with Tenny in tow.

The two women had not seen much of each other during the week. Caroline left early in the mornings and returned late at night. Each day she had carried a little more stress in her face. Her words had been a little less assured. Her gaze met Tenny's fewer and fewer times. Tenny had known that Caroline was not "skating" this time. This journey was all uphill on skis, unable to move directly forward, each step frustratingly small and the progress not comparable to the effort.

Then it seemed as if she had reached the top. Caroline suddenly gave the impression that she had accomplished her task and was ready to enjoy its results. But instead she was throwing herself into her day of relaxation, almost like she was trying to escape. They explored more Wright homes and buildings. They visited museums and Wrigley Field.

As they meandered down the Magnificent Mile, Tenny said, "After growing up in California, you can imagine what a shock it was when the FBI assigned me to the Atlanta office. If it hadn't been a big city, I would have definitely lost my mind. At least most big cities have enough diversity to make them bearable. You know what I mean, though — shit, you grew up in the biggest of them all."

"Yeah, but New York is in a class all by itself." Caroline sighed.

"Well, anyway, I didn't last long in Atlanta or the FBI. Local law enforcement is really what I was meant to do. It's so rewarding. Sometimes you can actually see how you've helped. That's a rare thing, and that's why I do it." Tenny caught herself almost instantly and looked away from Caroline. She pursed her lips and set her jaw, then she crossed her arms. Suddenly Tenny felt lost; she had given up so much. She had given up so much, and they still might not find Kelsey or stop the Jenkinses. Caroline pushed the idea from her head.

She and Caroline had been having such a nice conversation all day, learning about each other's youth, sharing their discovery of public service. Devoted to their careers, they were two separate people from two different backgrounds, with two different motivations. Caroline's name was deceiving. She was actually from a low-income, blue-collar family in which love was a luxury. Her motivation had always been to create more for herself and to protect the children — something she had tried to do for herself and her sisters as they grew up but never quite had the ability. Now she did, and she ruthlessly prosecuted those who dared to harm children. Tenny, on the other hand, was raised in an upper-middle-class home that was always filled with love. She had seen all that was right about the world. But the knowledge that not everyone was as fortunate motivated her to try to change that inequity.

The sun began to drop and Moose was now the one being dragged. Caroline stopped and hugged her best friend. "I think Moose has had enough. It'll get cold really fast." She stood. "I think tonight will be a perfect night for a picnic in front of the fireplace. It's Moose's favorite way to spend an evening. What do you think?"

Tenny smiled. "It sounds wonderful."

"Great! We'll stop at the store on the way home and

pick up a few things." She started back toward the car. "Now, let's see, what should I make? Chicken? Nah, it's an overused picnic main course. Hmm, giant shrimp?"

Tenny grimaced.

"I guess shrimp is out. Ah, I know! Oh yeah, yeah, that's good." Caroline was gone, escaping from the city street and into her world where there was no pain, dirtiness or fear, only food and creating. Tenny followed and eavesdropped as Caroline intently discussed the menu with Moose.

"So, tell me about Carter," Caroline casually inquired. They were sipping wine as they sat propped against the couch talking quietly in only the firelight.

Tenny forgot that she had even mentioned Carter. She must have mentioned her while telling Caroline about Pearl, and how it felt when she found Angelica. Disbelief swept through her as she realized how much she had told this woman. It was so easy. Each of Tenny's divulging truths had been reciprocated by Caroline, and already Tenny felt closer to her than anybody in her life since Carter. She hadn't even talked about some of this with Ashley and Steve.

"She's not a topic I usually discuss." Tenny thought this openness had to have its limits.

"All right, what do you want to talk about?" Caroline didn't seem to mind.

"How about we just sit here and listen to Moose snore." Tenny grinned as she nudged Moose with her toe and the Dane moaned in her sleep.

They sat still in the quiet for several minutes. But thoughts of Carter invaded Tenny's mind. She kept flashing through their lives together and apart. The first time they met. The feel of their first kiss. The joy of the three of them being a family. The pain when they had said good-bye forever. The moment she saw Carter again, and the empty shell Carter appeared to be without her daughter.

"Carter was probably the best thing that ever happened in my life. I loved her so much and I knew that she loved me. We were good for each other." Tenny started to speak half-unconsciously. "I wanted to spend the rest of my life with them." Tenny stared at the wall, lost in her memories.

Caroline gently brought her back. "Why didn't you?"

Tenny continued softly, "I don't know. I don't know what happened. It all went to hell so fast after Pearl was murdered." Her hands clenched into fists, bolting her to the floor and preventing her from fleeing. "I guess I lost confidence in life. I no longer believed in good prevailing over bad. I couldn't trust that anything was forever." She gave a sarcastic laugh. "I'd been in law enforcement for years and I still believed in those things. No wonder my little fantasy world disintegrated when reality gave me a good slap in the face. She did what she had to do for herself and Kelsey." Tenny was gathering herself, "I was negative, afraid. Carter didn't leave me because she didn't love me anymore. She'd lost me." Tenny took one huge breath. "What about your husband?"

"Nothing dramatic there." Caroline spoke quickly, without emotion. "We were married for three years. He got a promotion in his corporation and had to move to Texas. I was going to move as soon as I could find a comparable position down there." Caroline started to gather the empty plates and glasses. "It took less than a month for the distance to destroy three years of marriage. I guess that doesn't say much for this love thing, huh?" The last comment was tersely tossed over her shoulder as she left the room.

When she came back, Tenny had moved closer to the

warmth of the fire, lying in front of it with her head propped on her hand. Moose was stretched out with her back tucked up against her. Caroline stepped over Tenny's body and lay down, resting her head comfortably on Tenny's waist. The muscles in Tenny's body tightened.

Tenny felt awkward being close to this woman, yet how they shared physical space and protected emotions also seemed strangely comfortable to her. There were no unspoken expectations. There were no hidden agendas behind the questions. They were only two women totally enjoying each other's company. Tenny had never considered a relationship with this type of closeness and no romance. It felt good.

"You know, Tenny, we can't hide from love forever." Caroline smiled. "It's time that we accept that love is not a one-time thing. It's not invulnerable. It's not something magical. It's not something that can be created. It's most definitely not something to figure out and manipulate."

Tenny laughed nervously. "Oh, so now you're the expert."

"I wish I were." Caroline sighed. "I think love is like a rare flower. This flower is so rare because it's extremely difficult to grow. Nobody has ever really discovered when it should be planted, or what type of soil is best, or where the best environment is for the flower, or exactly how much water it needs. When it does flourish, nobody really knows why." Caroline continued, "Sometimes it just springs from the ground out of nowhere. Sometimes it's purposely planted, and much patience and care goes into cultivating it. Either way, sometimes the flower won't grow. Then, sometimes it grows a little but then can't withstand its environment and dies. Some of these flowers live for years, but the damn things won't ever bloom. Then other times they bloom over and over again, but an uncontrollable factor destroys them."

Tenny was silent.

Caroline started to tap the tile near the fire to emphasize her point. "The important thing is that people keep trying to nurture these flowers, because the pleasure they bring is worth the effort."

They both were quiet. The only movement in the room was the shadows of the flames. It all seemed so simple.

After a while Caroline asked, "Are you asleep?"

"How could I sleep with all the coffee you pumped into me this afternoon?" Still, the wine was beginning to take effect and Tenny was more relaxed. "I was thinking about flowers."

Caroline laughed gently. "We're lucky."

"Why's that?"

"Because we can share, give and trust without having to worry about whether our flower's going to bloom and survive." Caroline paused and Tenny finished the thought as naturally as if it had been her own.

"That's because friendships are like weeds. They survive just about everything and grow out of control." At that, they laughed so hard that they woke Moose, who groaned and moved off to another room for some peace and quiet.

The comfortable feeling of the night before vanished with the darkness which had helped to create it. A silent strain descended upon them the next morning at the kitchen table. Caroline rose to leave for work. "I'll call you as soon as I hear."

Tenny had her articles out again, and the one on the top of the stack reported on Tom Jenkins's rare coin collection, which was thought to be one of the most extensive in the country. He had inherited it from his father, along with the enthusiasm for trading and

132

treasuring rare things. According to the article, Jenkins traveled throughout the nation to attend coin shows.

Caroline grazed Tenny's shoulder, and Tenny grabbed her hand. "Your buddy at the IRS isn't going to find anything." She gestured to the article as if it was a key piece of evidence. "He's hidden the money here. They use those coins as an effective cover for their travels and money. Maybe everyone was right. Maybe they can't be touched."

"My friend may be able to help us establish a pattern of purchases above and beyond their income." Caroline tried to sound confident. Tenny knew this would require an audit which the IRS was not going to do unless they had a damn good reason to suspect some type of fraud. "I'll call you."

Pacing in front of the gate, Caroline was trying to calm down before Tenny arrived. When she had called the house, there had been no answer. Caroline hadn't even bothered to go by and check the house. After calling and getting the time of the next flight to San Francisco, she had driven directly out to the airport. Caroline had seen Tenny's airline tickets and knew which carrier she was traveling on. There was still an hour before the flight left.

Caroline couldn't believe how hurt she felt by Tenny's actions. The friendship which had seemed so natural and strong suddenly seemed worthless. Why hadn't Tenny waited to talk to her before leaving? Maybe they could have thought of more options together. Maybe they could have found another way to approach this search. Why did she have to leave? It wasn't over yet. Caroline stopped pacing, a question temporarily deflecting her anger. Was she upset about the investigation or about losing a friend?

"What's brought you here?" Tenny's voice drifted to Caroline from behind.

She spun, all her anger instantly returning. "What are you doing? Were you just going to leave? Just like that?"

"My search is over." Tenny clenched her teeth as her throat tightened around a lump of sorrow. Her eyelids grew heavy. She shoved her hand in her pants' pockets. "There's nothing left for me to do. I have to go home and tell Carter that I failed, that her baby's not coming home."

Caroline tried to reassure her. "I've only started. Why don't you give me a chance?"

Tenny sounded tired. "It's over. There's nothing left."

Caroline was hurt. "So that's it."

"What more is there?"

Caroline started to walk away. "Good-bye would have been nice."

Chapter Seventeen

The last week of October and the beginning of November had been an agonizing time. After leaving Chicago, Tenny had intended to tell Carter that there was nothing more she could do. Then she was going to try to get her life in order. But when she had arrived home, she had been paralyzed by doubt.

Had she done everything that she could? Could she sleep through a night, or wake up in the morning without thinking of Kelsey? Could she ever really move on? These questions had haunted her until she had realized that it wasn't over — yet.

There was one more option for Tenny. It required that she give up all chances of ever stepping into her role as an officer again. It meant forsaking all the rules and laws that she had lived by for years. It would result in a revolution of thought, even if it was only Tenny's. She bought another ticket to Chicago.

She hated snow, but this morning she had been forced to walk what seemed like a few miles in it. There was no way she was going to attempt to drive on the slick streets. A taxi dropped her at a small shopping center. The walk had actually given her an opportunity to plan her break-in. The Jenkinses were at work. A simple call to their respective offices had confirmed that they both had full schedules today. The polite receptionist unknowingly assisted her as she answered a few questions for a prospective client.

The house was undoubtedly alarmed. If those damn coins were kept in the house, it was probably better armed than the Getty Museum. Cutting the electricity would solve the problem of multiple alarms, but the initial power loss would set off a systems alarm. Any decent cop checking the place would notice the stopped or flashing clocks. Further inspection might lead to the cut electricity and then she'd be in trouble. Tenny decided against it. Instead, she decided to look for a way to the second floor, where she could make her entry.

She would trigger an alarm, but if the cops found the ground floor secure, hopefully they would only perform a visual check of the second-floor windows and doors. What she really had to worry about were neighbors who might happen to glance out a window and see her scaling the side of the house.

She looked up from the snow. One patch of snow seemed as treacherous as the next. She stood in front of the house next to the Jenkinses'. The neighbors didn't appear to be home, although with the size of the houses it was difficult to tell. Casually she strolled by the Jenkinses' and checked the other neighbors. Empty, as far as she could tell.

Tenny returned to the center house and quickly ducked into the yard, which meant climbing a tall iron gate. She thanked the Jenkinses for being a little excessive. A solid wooden gate would have prevented her from getting in. The brick wall surrounding the yard was at least seven feet tall — difficult to scale.

Once in the yard, Tenny relaxed somewhat. Nobody could see her and there wasn't much of a threat — unless, unless . . . Tenny froze. She had forgotten this possibility. Slowly, very slowly, she started to look around without moving anything but her head. What if there was a dog? Nothing, no growling, barking or the sound of paws charging at her through the snow. Any decent guard dog would have been on her before she even made it over the gate. Of course.

She circled the house, looking for the best place to gain access to the upper floor. She tried the downstairs doors and windows. Maybe she would get lucky. People with alarm systems often got lazy and careless.

"Yes! Yes!" Tenny found a French door that could be forced open. It was locked, but the latch throw was so shallow that a good push would open the door without doing any damage or indicating that somebody had entered. Tenny reviewed her plan again before setting off the alarm.

If this police department was any good, she'd have two to three minutes to find a place to hide. It would have to be a good place, because the cops would either force their way in the same way she did or ask for somebody with a key to respond. In addition, there were probably motion detectors inside which she would also set off as she moved through the house. Hopefully, once the alarm company informed the police of the perimeter alarm, they wouldn't bother to call back and update the information about interior movement. It was important information for cops, but the techs at alarm companies didn't have any incentive to be thorough. They figured they had done their job, now it was the cops' problem.

Tenny pushed the door. The blaring horn was deafening. She glanced back at the yard as she was about to enter. "Shit! Shit! How could I be so stupid." Tenny's footprints were nicely captured in the snow near the house. No fucking cop could miss those. She had no choice.

Tenny jumped off the porch area and sprinted across the yard to the back wall and jumped up, knocking snow from the top. Then she turned and carefully started to step backward through her prints. It was taking too long. She was running out of time. By the time she reached the porch again, at least three minutes had passed. Her time was almost up.

A loud engine accelerated around the corner. Tenny knew that sound. Cops all over the country drove the same cars and the noise they made was identical. She quickly slipped out of her shoes, wrapped them in her shirt, closed the door behind her and darted into the house. "Where are the goddamned stairs? Fuck this damn house!" She was searching for the stairs but in her panic she had gotten turned around. She couldn't even figure out the way to the front of the house.

From outside she heard a door slam. Bad officer safety, but at least Tenny knew that an officer was approaching the house. She was out of time.

The stairs suddenly appeared out of nowhere. "Thank you, Lord." She went to the first closet she could find. "Perfect!" The panel across the crawlspace moved easily, and she hoisted herself through. Then she leaned out and pulled the closet door shut and replaced the panel. She held her hands over her ears. Tenny's head felt like it was about to burst as the alarm pierced every wall of the house.

Twenty minutes later the alarm reset. Tenny waited quietly. She had not been able to hear anything while the alarm was sounding. For all she knew, the cops had already entered, checked the house and left. Or they could be waiting outside for somebody to bring a key. They could be inside the house right now. She wondered what they thought of her footprints. Considering what she would have done with a set of prints indicating that at the least somebody had been prowling around the house, Tenny knew she was in trouble. She made an awful crook.

After a few moments Tenny's heart sank at what she heard next. "Police! We have a dog! Come out with your hands up or we'll send the dog in." Tenny held her spot. They could be bluffing. There was no evidence to indicate that she had actually made it in. The alarm could have been set off by somebody trying to get in. They were only covering their asses. Tenny closed her eyes and hoped they were bluffing.

The same booming voice was speaking to the other officers now. "Bring the K-9 up." In a few moments she could hear the police dog whining with excitement at the front door. The handler gave the dog some orders in German and then it began to bark wildly. Even if she had wanted to give up, there was no way she was coming down with that monster running loose. Anyway, she had one more hope.

In her confused attempt to find the stairs she had been all over the lower floor. Crossing her paths repeatedly, backtracking, turning, stopping. Her scent downstairs had to be a mess. The K-9 might be so distracted by her lost wanderings that it wouldn't hit on the stairs. It might be so misguided that its handler would think it wasn't really hitting on anything. Tenny listened as the dog scrambled around downstairs.

"Nope. I don't think we've got anything in here. He was hitting much better on the wall outside." The handler had given up.

"There are no prints on the other side of that wall. What'd he do, vanish at the damn wall?" The other officer wasn't easily fooled.

"I don't know about that. All I know is that my partner isn't hitting on anything inside the house." The K-9 handler was annoyed. He was also wrong.

"Fine. Tommy, I want you and Bert to check this house. I mean check it, too. Under beds, closets, attic, basement, all of it. Every fucking square inch."

Tenny knew that once the orders were given the supervisor would leave. Then she would find out how thorough Tommy and Bert were. It seemed like it took hours before she heard one of the officers yank open the closet door. The hangers squeaked as the officer shoved the clothes aside. Then the door shut again. Finally, Tenny relaxed. Her heart was still racing, but she knew she was going to be all right. That wasn't so hard, she thought to herself and smiled.

Tenny eased out of the crawlspace after she was sure the police had left. She cracked the door and searched the room for motion detectors. The cops wouldn't miss her again if they got another alarm at this address. The room was clear and she stepped out of the closet. The clock in the room told her it was just after one in the afternoon. She would have hours to conduct her search. She removed a pillow case from a closet. Tenny wanted to make sure the cops knew that somebody had been here. Maybe they would be more careful in the future. She would make it look like a routine burglary and then dump the property somewhere. Tenny didn't want any of their possessions.

What she really sought were clues to where the children were — to find out where Kelsey could be found.

It was dark by the time Tenny got back to the hotel. She ran hot water into the tub and collapsed into the soothing warmth. The fear, adrenaline and fatigue had taken its toll. She was exhausted. Worse, she was frustrated. All her efforts had been for nothing. All she had come away with was a bag of valuables that meant nothing, a small key which she had discovered hidden in the library and a picture of their son when he was young which she'd removed from a photo album in the bedroom. She didn't even know why she had taken it.

She assumed that the key was to a safe deposit box, but she had no idea where. She had written down the names of every financial institution she'd found on documents in the house. She counted them now — fifteen. It would take forever to track down the box, if she even could. Banks weren't extremely cooperative with providing information, not even to the police. Of course, Tenny wasn't a cop anymore. Today she had ended that part of her life forever.

Maybe she could ask Caroline for help. But she hadn't even let her friend know that she was back. She couldn't involve anybody else in her search. They all had so much to lose — everything which she'd already thrown away. She missed Caroline, but she couldn't allow her to take any chances. Caroline was too valuable an asset to have on the side of the system. Tomorrow Tenny would finish, alone.

The alarm code, which she had found during her hunt, made her escape easy. It would also allow her reentry without the chaos of today. When she went back, she

141

would be quiet. That would be important because the next time the house would not be empty. She wanted answers and she intended to get them.

Tenny allowed her body to slide beneath the water until the warmth was up to her neck. She closed her eyes and tried to concentrate. For a moment she saw nothing; her mind was surrendering to sleep. Then the face came out of the darkness. As the face drew closer, Tenny tensed. "Oh shit!"

It was a face she knew. She had seen it before. Before learning about the Jenkinses or coming to Chicago. Stumbling from the tub, she grabbed a towel and wrapped it around her without bothering to dry off. Rushing out to her room, she snatched the briefcase which held all the articles she had collected from the beginning. She knew that face.

Chapter Eighteen

The child was stretching back over his shoulder. Reaching, straining and in desperate need of help. The child was silent although her eyes pleaded for Tenny to save her. Then suddenly Tenny felt a grasp. Pearl's hand closed around her own and there was the touch that Tenny had never been able to rid from her body. But instead of Pearl's face, it was her granddaughter, telling Tenny again how her sister died. A child! A child! They were getting away with the children!

Tenny threw out her arms to take the child back and

they crashed into the lamp on the hotel bed's nightstand. The pain and the crash startled her from her nightmare. For several minutes she sat breathless and dizzy on the side of her bed. The fluorescent green numerals in the clock read one o'clock in the morning. Time for Tenny to get ready to keep a promise.

She went to her suitcase and took out the steel gun box. This was her personal gun that she had bought as a rookie FBI agent. Back then, she had been a twenty-four-hour cop and had carried it everywhere. But as she matured in law enforcement, she learned to rely less on a weapon and more on her intellect. She had almost forgotten she owned a gun. The use of the weapon would carry her further and further from the law which she respected. But maybe it would also bring her closer to the child she loved.

"What the shit!" As Tom Jenkins sat up in his bed, his chest met a sharp blow from Tenny's hand. Jenkins bounced back down to his pillow. Tenny was kneeling between him and his wife on their bed. The gun was inches from his wife's face. He seemed as if he was about to demand an explanation, but he remained quiet.

Tenny was back and she wanted answers. She wore no gloves, no mask, nothing to conceal her identity. She was not a criminal and she wasn't going to hide. "I want to know where Kelsey Sabatos is. If you tell me, then you live. If not, then one of you will watch the other die."

"Who are you?" Anne Jenkins was cool, as if she were the one with the control.

"That doesn't really matter. I know that you paid somebody to snatch a child and then you sold that child. I want to know who you sold her to." Tenny tried to match

Anne Jenkins's composure, although Tenny felt more desperate than calm.

The woman reached out and turned on the bedside lamp. Tenny made no move to stop her. "I recognize you from somewhere." Jenkins squinted as if to get a better look at the woman kneeling only an arm's distance away.

Her husband filled the silent void. "We don't know what you're talking about." He was doing an admirable performance of appearing confused. "We don't know anything about stolen children. In fact, we're big supporters of the work being done to end child abductions in this country."

Tenny twisted toward him. For a moment she wanted to strike him. Her grip became so tight that the tension was causing the gun to vibrate in her grasp. "You do know what I'm talking about and I have the evidence to prove it."

Anne slowly let a smile creep to her lips. "You talk like a cop. Is this how police work is done in California, Officer?"

Tenny sighed; she knew that there would be a chance that they remembered. So many people could recall every contact that they had ever had with the police. Why should these two be any different?

"I'm not an officer anymore. I've stepped into your world and I plan to show you the same type of concern which you've shown for all those children." Tenny tried to communicate a deadly intention. "I'm only going to ask once more — where is Kelsey?" There was no persuasion in her voice, only promise.

"You claim to have evidence against us. Bring us up on charges and find out where she is yourself." Tom Jenkins tested her patience. "You don't have shit!"

Tenny stared at him as she reached into her jacket pocket. "Here's my evidence, asshole." She tossed the newspaper article onto his chest. It was about a kidnapping of a small boy from a farming community in Illinois. The boy was six at the time, twelve years ago. He grinned from under the front-page caption announcing his abduction.

"So, what's this? What's it got to do with us?" Jenkins's voice was shaking and his wife wouldn't even look at the article.

It was Tenny's turn to smirk. She reached back into her pocket and removed the picture of their son, taken during the burglary. It had looked familiar for a good reason.

Tenny threw it to the bed between them. "Those two little boys could be twins, don't you think?" Neither Jenkins would look at the photograph. "In fact, they could be the same little boy. What do you think?"

Anne Jenkins seemed unshaken. "I'll tell you everything. There's nothing you can do to us with the knowledge. There's nothing you can do to us."

Why was this woman still so confident? Tenny sensed that she had made another terrible mistake.

"It started with our first, when we took our son. We wanted a child, but not a baby. All the older children up for adoption were unacceptable for various reasons. Therefore we found our own child and he was perfect." Anne Jenkins spoke as if she were delivering a lecture. "It was so easy. We thought that there had to be many people like us that wanted children. We knew we could provide them with their own perfect child."

Tenny kept the gun level as Anne Jenkins spoke.

"Of course at first there were problems, just like any new business. We didn't have efficient control over the selection process and too many criminal losers were taking too many children. In the early nineteen eighties we thought the whole thing was going to fall apart. When that asshole killed Adam Walsh and didn't get rid of the body, we were sure our business had been short-lived. Adam's

146

father became a champion for missing children and the media got hooked, which dragged the government into the whole thing. It was getting quite impossible."

Tom Jenkins smiled and proverbalized, "Ah yes, but to each problem there is a solution."

Anne grinned back. They were taunting her, Tenny knew. "Indeed, a few well-planned dinner parties with the appropriate guest and an intellectual discussion of the child abduction crisis. Soon the media was sending a different message. Instead of an epidemic, the nation was facing a social construction problem, built up by media sensationalism. The 'experts' began researching the numbers and announcing things like 'the number gap' and 'misleading statistics.' The FBI even took our side, although quite by accident, when they began to downplay the numbers of actual stranger abductions."

"Oh, my favorite was the article, 'The Myth and Fear of Child Abduction.' That one really shot up the numbers," Tom said. Tenny felt sick. She had read all those articles. The authors probably never even suspected that they were being used.

"It didn't take long for the hysteria to pass. Now it only surfaces every once in a while when an abduction draws unusual media attention for some reason. Unfortunately, we can't control what the people who steal the children do and sometimes they are not as professional as we would like. Currently we're developing a method of dealing with that also. Anyway, these days the attention is usually local and brief. There's always a bigger story to tell." She paused to let the information, the truth, sink in. "Tom handles the paperwork and produces perfect fraudulent documents. The children are healthy and exactly what parents want, and they do pay well. Our customers don't know how we get the children and don't want to know."

Tenny couldn't believe how calm this woman acted. It

147

was all so sinister, but she made it sound so simple. Tenny tried to focus. "I want to know where Kelsey is!"

"That, my dear, we're not going to tell you." Anne Jenkins was smug.

"Oh yes, you will!" Tenny's frustration was exploding. "You tell me where she is or I'll tell your precious son who he really is! Fuck the courts! I'll show him who his parents really are and what they've been doing."

The laughter from the Jenkinses haunted her. She had thrown out her ace and they were laughing at her. Instantly she knew that all the warnings she'd been given, the advice she'd chosen not to take, the tempered approach which she'd tossed aside had been right. Tenacity was not going to prevail this time.

Anne Jenkins continued to humor her. "Our son was kidnapped in the state of Illinois and he never crossed any state line during that crime. That means it's not a federal crime. The six-year statute of limitations is long past. As for your telling our son, really, Officer, who do you think he will trust?"

Tenny struggled. "It's not a matter of trust. The article is all the proof he'll need."

"Oh really, did you really think that we hadn't prepared an explanation years ago?" Anne was condescending. "Would you like to hear the truth?"

Tenny finally lowered the gun, sat back from her kneeling stance and prepared herself for the story that she knew she'd never be able to discredit.

"We found our son in a deserted camping area. He had been beaten and was near death. Although his face was distorted with swelling and discoloration, we recognized him as the small boy who had tragically been taken from his home. We tried to take him home, but discovered that soon after his abduction his parents had been killed in a horrible car accident. So I nursed him back to health and my husband and I decided to just keep him."

Tenny understood. "You had his parents killed."

Again she smiled. "Of course not. It was a Shakespearean coincidence." There was no statute of limitations for murder. Tenny looked at the weapon in her hand as Anne Jenkins continued. "We felt that in his best interest it would be better if his true identity was never known so that the media wouldn't forever follow his every step. Therefore Tom created some fictitious documents and some friends of mine in the Social Services Department helped us to adopt him. What you may be able to prove, Officer, is forgery of state documents, but really, would anybody with a heart blame us for protecting a child that had already been through so much?"

Tenny had no more options. She thrust the gun into the woman's face. "Tell me where Kelsey is! Tell me now or you fucking die!"

She didn't flinch. Her voice was steady. "Officer, I'm unarmed."

Tenny had to end this game. She had to kill her so the spineless husband would tell her what she must know. The pressure on the trigger began to increase. There were no more choices, no more chances, no more clues. There was only one path to the answer she sought. The trigger began to creep back.

You've crossed the line. Her captain's words echoed around her. She couldn't do it. She couldn't cross this line.

"I'll be there. Everywhere you go from now until I die. I'll be there and I'll be watching. This is not over!" Tenny withdrew, returning to the darkness of the night.

"Listen carefully, there's a problem." It was Tom Jenkins. He placed the call on his cellular phone minutes after Caroline saw a dark figure flee from his yard.

"Let me guess. Elizabeth?" The voice sounded Hispanic.

149

"What? I don't know what you're talking about! Just know that you may want to be careful for a while. I assure you that we will deal with this problem." Jenkins was clearly in control.

"Be sure that you do." The line was disconnected.

Caroline set the scanner down and started to pack up her stuff. "I'm out of here." She thought she had everything she'd need. Then suddenly Tom Jenkins's voice filled the van again.

"I have a job for you." The conversation which she overheard this time made her heart race. ". . . and take care of them all if you have to." The line went dead again.

That morning, Caroline had read a small piece in the daily paper about a burglary at the Jenkins home. Instantly she knew that her friend was back in town. Caroline hadn't given up and guessed what Tenny's next step would be. She made plans to take advantage of it.

Caroline had cut the telephone wires while Tenny was inside. She anticipated that Jenkins would be panicked enough by his late-night visitor to make a critical mistake, and he had. She captured the international call placed with operator assistance. Evidence which would be admissible. But more importantly, she now had the piece that Tenny sought. A single telephone number which would lead to the most precious evidence of all — Kelsey.

Chapter Nineteen

The water was scorching Tenny's body as it pounded down on her from the shower head. But she felt nothing. Her skin was numbed by the reality of her failure. She found herself unable to focus on anything. Her mind blitzed through all her painful memories, her shortcomings, her unkept promises. She had risked everything, but there was nothing left this time. She shut off the shower and began to laugh at her imprudence. "You finally fell for all this Tenacity bullshit and look where it got you."

It had taken her all morning to simply get out of bed.

Alone, she didn't have to explain to anybody. She didn't have to think at all, if she could only make herself sleep.

Rest would not come and finally Tenny had forced herself to finish this part of her life. Now, she quickly dressed and threw things into her carry-on bag. She just wanted to end it. Fly back and tell Carter that she had been beaten by the Jenkinses. They were never going to tell anybody where Kelsey had been taken. Kelsey was the one piece of evidence that could destroy them. The children that had been taken could never be found alive. At least Tenny could tell her that she was sure that Kelsey was alive and living with a family. Maybe she was even somewhat happy. In that respect, Kelsey had been lucky. It was something to offer. Tenny knew that it wasn't enough.

After she told Carter, she was going to leave everything behind, not that she had much. She had no job. She had no partner. She couldn't afford her house anymore and it had never been her home. Her family and friends would understand. Tenacity was going to disappear, and maybe Elizabeth could find herself again. Maybe!

Tenny dropped the room key through the express checkout slot and headed out to the freezing streets. She didn't bother to put her jacket on. The intense heat had not affected her, nor would the chill.

A taxi pulled up to the front of the hotel as Tenny exited. The curb door swung open and Caroline stepped out. For a moment Tenny wanted to rush into her arms and cry until the tears wouldn't come anymore. But her next instinct was to turn and walk away, keeping her pain to herself. Instead, Tenny stopped and just looked at her.

"Hi there," Caroline said tentatively. "I had a feeling you were back in town. You forgot to come by and say hello. I don't know if Moose will ever get over it." Caroline smiled.

Tenny didn't respond. Caroline walked up and shoved two round-trip tickets at her. Tenny's hand felt like it belonged on a corpse.

"Put your jacket on, stupid, this isn't California." She pointed to the tickets. "That's where Kelsey is."

For a long moment the words Tenny heard made no sense. She gripped the tickets until they crumpled somewhat.

"We both know that she's alive and she's waiting for you to come get her. Tenny, she needs you. Damn it, go get her and bring her home!"

Tenny looked down at the tickets in her hand. She had one more chance. This time there would be no mistakes. "Why two tickets?" Her mind was slowly starting to function again.

As if on cue, the door to the taxi opened again and Carter stepped out. Tenny caught her breath as Carter rushed past Caroline and took Tenny into her arms. They held each other for a long time.

"I called your Mom. I knew something was going on, but I hadn't heard anything," Carter was explaining. "I got Caroline's number and she told me everything." She pulled Tenny tighter. "I'm going with you. I'm not going to let you do this alone this time. We're going to get *our* baby back."

Caroline said, "Okay, you two need to get going. I made an appointment at the consulate for you to get visas, and you'll have to stop at the bank. Your plane leaves in three hours, so let's get going."

Tenny was still trying to keep up. "I don't have my passport or enough clothes."

Carter smiled sheepishly. "Well, I still have my key. You haven't moved anything around. I have everything you'll need."

Tenny looked at her. "You kept your key?" But she didn't wait for an answer. She turned to Caroline. "How did you get this information?"

Caroline kept her moving toward the taxi. "Don't worry about that, I was careful." She looked smug. "I monitored a call he made by cell phone on a scanner. Perfectly legal to use in court, Tenny. I'm going to bring them down." Caroline was pushing them into the cab, and then suddenly she hooked Tenny's arm and dragged her back out. "You need to be cautious. All three of you are in danger. They didn't just warn the family. There'll be another person searching for Kelsey. But his orders have nothing to do with saving her."

Tenny understood. "Thanks." Tenny dug into her pocket and brought out a copy of the safe deposit key which she had taken from the Jenkinses. Last night she had replaced it so they wouldn't notice it missing. "Here, take this. I don't think it'll do you any good for the moment, but promise me that if we don't come back, you'll find a way to put an end to what they're doing. Promise me that!"

Caroline took the key. "I intend to bring them down. And you are *all* coming back."

Tenny got into the taxi with Carter and looked at the tickets. "Rio de Janeiro, Brazil." She was stunned.

BOOK THREE

Chapter Twenty

"Did you know that Brazil is the fifth largest nation in the world?" Carter had two pillows propped against the armrest separating her from Tenny and was lying on her back with her knees resting against the two seats which she was occupying. Tenny knew she wasn't sleeping. "It's bigger than the continental United States. Its coast is forty-six hundred miles and the longest in the world. It has two of the largest cities in the world, Rio de Janeiro and São Paulo."

Carter reached back over her head without ever opening her eyes. She found one of the three books sitting open on Tenny's meal tray. "Why don't you close that thing and try to get some rest. In another six hours you'll be able to learn everything you've ever wanted to know about Brazil first hand."

"No, we have to be prepared." Tenny had never really understood how Carter could approach life in such a carefree manner. "I mean we know nothing about the country. The more we know, the better we're able to operate there and the greater chance we'll have of finding Kelsey."

Carter opened her eyes. "All right, tell me about Brazil."

"Oh, well there's so much. They speak Portuguese. In 1807 King Joao VI fled Portugal when Napoleon conquered it. The King went to Brazil and started its history of being just a little different from the rest of the world, by making Brazil the first and only colony to act as seat of government for the mother country." Tenny was spewing out the facts which she had already memorized.

"Elizabeth, I don't want to hear that stuff. Tell me about Brazil."

"That's what I was doing."

"No you were giving the tour guide version." Carter tilted her head back to look at Tenny. "Tell me about the country. Tell me why my daughter was taken there."

It was just like Carter to ask this question. She operated from the soul and not the head. Tenny knew that Carter would do fine in this country. Brazil was a country motivated by heart and soul. "Well, the economists of the world say *potential* is Brazil's middle name." Tenny started to explain, "After all, it has the world's sixth largest population and is the capitalist world's second largest consumer. It's the seventh largest steel producer in the world. The second largest in the production of iron ore. Plus, it's either one, two or three in several agricultural areas."

Tenny continued, but she was no longer reciting facts. Her words came more slowly and her tone softened. "Still,

Brazil is a poor country and a corrupt country. It's trapped between the first world and the third world."

"What about the people?" Carter sat up. "Why did they take my baby?" She made it sound as if the nation had committed the crime.

"It's complicated. I may be assuming too much from the information in these books." Tenny hesitated.

"When it comes to finding answers among words, you've always been the best." Carter seemed sincere. It was amazing how Tenny could discover the truth hidden in the mass of distracting and deceptive arguments.

"Well, I thought the United States had a distinctive history, but Brazil could easily be its sister." Tenny started her theory. "We share so much. The Native Indians that were threatened and almost destroyed by European settlers. The slaves which were brought from Africa to Brazil to do the white man's work while only the white man profited. Plus, we share the melting pot theory although in Brazil it is normally referred to as the *bleaching of Brazil*." Tenny and Carter both giggled a little at this thought. It was one indication of how the two countries were different.

Tenny continued, "Look, here's a quote: *Brazilians don't really know what color they are and many of them don't care either*." Tenny stopped for moment and looked around the plane. Then she leaned close to Carter and whispered, "Look at the people on this damn plane and tell me that color doesn't make a difference in Brazil."

When Carter looked she saw only white faces. Sure they were tanned from living in Brazil's climate, but their features were most definitely European. In fact, her daughter would fit in nicely with these people. Dark hair, beautiful brown eyes, and soft light skin which was easily browned by the sun.

Tenny began flipping through one of her books. "Now look at the pictures in this book." As the pages turned, Carter saw one dark face after another. The people captured were the Mamelucos, the Cafuso, and the Mulattos. Tenny went on, "They say that discrimination in Brazil is based more on economic status than on race, but it's not that simple. Not in their country and not in ours." Carter already understood, but Tenny concluded, "Something tells me that Kelsey is down here because she's the right color."

They sat quietly for a while, each considering the journey that lay before them. Carter noticed Tenny bending the edges of the thick paperback, the muscles in Tenny's arms working with much more force than required and straining with tension. Tenny's eyes were locked to the cover's photograph of Rio de Janeiro's Sugarloaf.

She touched Tenny's cheek. "It's going to be all right. We're going to find our Kelsey and take her home."

"How can you be so relaxed!" She hadn't meant to snap. "I'm sorry, but you seem so confident. We're going to be in a foreign country and we don't even speak their language. We don't know what's waiting for us and we won't have any help."

Carter sat back and smiled softly, as if untouched by Tenny's harshness, uncertainty, or words. "There is a reason people call you Tenacity."

Tenny ran her hands through her hair as she spoke. "You know that the whole Tenacity thing is bent all out of proportion. Shit, I'm human! I'm not this great, unbeatable investigator that everybody can count on." She looked at Carter. "People like to create heroes, but I'm not one."

Carter brought her head down to Tenny's shoulder. "Elizabeth." She paused to let the name sink in. "I know who *you* are." Carter touched her chest. "That's why I trust you and believe in you, and that's why people call you Tenacity."

There was a long silence as both women thought about the past, then finally Tenny spoke. "Look, something else all these books say is that Brazil is a dangerous place. Shit they have pages of warning and precautions for tourists."

Lifting the armrest, Carter snuggled closer to Tenny. "So? It's not like we aren't coming from one of the most dangerous countries in the world. We'll be fine. Get some rest."

Tenny closed her eyes, but knew that she would not sleep. Carter didn't know everything that Tenny did. They would not be searching alone in this mysterious country.

"Wake up gal, we're getting ready to land." Tenny gently brushed Carter's hair back from her tired eyes.

She stirred a little, but did not move. Carter had always been slow to wake. Tenny began to twist her shoulder from beneath Carter's head. "You've got to sit up and put your seatbelt on. Come on Carter." She groaned and removed her head. Her legs swung to the floor bringing her torso up into a sitting position with their momentum. Grudgingly Carter began to search for the ends of her seatbelt and as she did so she glanced out the window to see how close they really were.

The sight out of the plane's small window caused Carter to scrunch her face down into the porthole opening to take in all that she possibly could. "Oh, my God! It's amazing. There's so much city and water and green. It's like nothing I've ever seen." There was no fatigue left in Carter's voice or body. These were the type of situations in which Carter was most at ease. New places, new faces; Carter had no trouble improvising and Brazil sounded like her kind of place.

She reached back and grabbed Tenny's arm, pulling her towards the window which could barely accommodate one curious face, much less two. As she leaned over to squeeze her face in next to Carter's she thought to herself, *you've seen one big city you've seen them all.*

"Oh shit!" Tenny hadn't been ready for this.

There were jutting stone mountains, partially bare with

weathered rock and partially covered with green vegetation. There was the ocean stretching away to the south. Directly under them were bays and inlets with crisp white strips of sand separating the water from the buildings. The buildings themselves occupied any space which nature had not already claimed as her own. Finally above it all stood a statute of Christ with his arms spread wide, welcoming all to this country.

Tenny sat back in her seat, closed her eyes, took a deep breath, let it out, and quietly said the only thing that came to mind—"Brazil."

The bag bounced from the bed to the floor with a heavy thud, but Tenny didn't even stop to correct her toss which had been a bit too strong. She needed air. She needed to think. She had to figure out. how they were going to manage to find Kelsey in this country. A simple trip from the airport to their hotel had been a challenge. From the moment they had stepped from the customs area into the main lobby of the airport, Tenny had felt out of control and sorely out of place.

It had started when a group of men had rushed at them when they had passed the ropes and police which keep anxious family and friends back while waiting for passengers to exit the customs area. The men, in what looked like tan uniforms, had instantly recognized Tenny and Carter for tourists and were upon them. One came at them so fast that Tenny didn't even have time to think, she just reacted. He was urgently grabbing at her bag and saying something in Portuguese. Instead of her bag, he had received a quick, sharp blow to his chest. At first his look had been one of utter disbelief, but it quickly changed to anger as Carter grabbed Tenny and dragged her away. The police standing nearby, who seemed amused by the scene, were probably the only thing that had save Tenny from her first international blunder.

Then there had been getting a taxi, which wasn't too much of a problem. But they had not changed their American dollars to Brazilian cruzeiros. Their taxi driver had willingly taken the dollars and then hustled them into an awaiting cab. Only for Tenny to discover that the man who had met them at the cab was not the driver and had accepted her money for no other reason than to open her door and tell the driver where they were going. At least she had been relatively confident that she had heard "Sheraton" in the jumble of other words that floated from his lips.

Carter had appeared to find the whole experience entertaining. She had spent the whole drive trying to communicate with the driver with her high school Spanish and his broken English. This had angered Tenny. It was as if she thought they were here on some type of vacation, and not because her child had been stolen and sent to this country.

Now as Tenny stepped out onto their balcony, all these emotions had her head spinning. She needed to breathe, but even the air down here was different. It had a strange smell to it which Tenny couldn't place. Everything was so strange.

The first thing she noticed as she looked around, was that across from their four-star hotel the hill was crowded with shanty homes. Small boxes, crushed side by side, with tiny squared windows sharing the Sheraton's view. This country couldn't keep its classes properly separated.

Thoughts kept shooting through Tenny's mind, blinding her to the breathtaking view which the balcony provided. Tenny stood staring at one of the world's most famous beaches, but she saw nothing but the images haunting her head. There was Pearl looking up at her from the cold ground, smiling and reassuring. Next was a flash of Pearl's body as she sat all alone and dead in the alley in which Tenny had left her. Then came Angelica's strong, confident, and searching face. She had looked and talked so much like her grandmother.

Then Kelsey's face was next to Angelica's. They were swinging side by side and asking Tenny to promise. Promise them that she would always be there. Promise that she would always find them. Promise. Promise. Promise. Tenny shut her eyes to get the images to leave her mind. In the darkness, a voice came, whispering, "I'll love you. What we have is forever, right now." Forever. Forever. Forever. She and Carter were in bed. They were in love. They were together. The tears began to pour over Tenny's cheeks, draining with them the memories.

"You all right." Carter didn't move to be near her. Tenny knew that Carter already had sensed her emotions. She had always known what Tenny was feeling, sometimes even before Tenny knew.

Tenny reached up and brushed her hair back, quickly wiping the tears away also. As if she could hide her tears from Carter. Still Tenny did not turn. "I'm scared to death. I don't know if I'm going to be able to find her."

"You will." There was no doubt in Carter's voice.

"How can you be so sure?" Tenny began to get angry again. It wasn't fair for Carter to put so much confidence in her abilities. It was too much pressure.

"Because it's time that something worked out right for us. It's time." Tenny couldn't miss the choked words as Carter finished.

The tears were gushing from Tenny's eyes when she finally turned to face Carter and saw Carter's own tears dripping to her folded arms. All Tenny could get out was "Why?" One word containing so many questions. Why did you leave? Why weren't you there for me? Why did you turn to that other woman? Why did you let love escape?

Those questions didn't have to be spoken. After losing

164

their love, both women had asked themselves these same questions and hundreds of others. Carter could barely speak as her tears turned to sobs. "I never stopped loving you. I just didn't know how to love you anymore. You were so closed, so lonely, motivated through life by something much bigger than our love. Then after Pearl, you set out on a mission that I didn't understand and which I couldn't follow."

Tenny stepped closer to Carter, but still they did not touch. Both breathed deeply, struggling to control their tears. After a moment, Tenny reached out with a trembling hand and let one finger lightly run down Carter's forearm which remained firmly crossed over her other arm. "I needed you." Tenny was almost whispering.

Carter stepped away. The touch was too much. "You needed me as an excuse not to chase away your nightmares and pursue your dreams. Our love was your weight and I couldn't bear that." Carter looked away.

Tenny moved forward and slowly reached out, but Carter again backed off. Tenny loved this woman. Tenny wanted this woman, like nothing she had ever wanted before. "I love you."

Carter brought her hands to her face and sobbed into them, "I know."

Tenny said it again. "I love you." Suddenly it was so plain. She loved this woman and that had never changed.

"I know!"

"You just said you still loved me, that you never stopped loving me." Tenny reached out and grasped Carter's hips while her face was concealed by her hands.

"I do love you." As Tenny gently tried to pull her close, Carter resisted. "Don't you see that's the problem! I do love you."

Tenny tugged harder and finally Carter came into her arms and instantly their bodies pressed firmly against each other. It was as if no time had passed, as they slid easily

165

together like so many times before. They clung to each other and cried, until Tenny finally brought Carter's head from her shoulder. For a long moment she just looked into Carter's eyes which shone with the ageless beauty of petrified wood. Tenny knew that this was the woman she loved. The only woman she would ever love.

Tilting her head to just the right angle, which her memory seemed to have programmed her body to find, Tenny's lips sought Carter's. At first she let her lips simply rest on Carter's and Tenny took a deep breath through her nose, remembering how good her lover smelled. Carter couldn't stand it any longer, and she grabbed the back of Tenny's neck and kissed her fully. Years of lost passion finally recovered. The kisses grew harder, longer, and wetter. Their grasp around each others body became stronger, forcing their bodies still closer.

Finally, Carter pulled her head back and they both glanced at the bed. They both laughed as they realized that they had both had the same thought. But the bed seemed so far away. Neither wanted to risk losing each other again. Unwilling to let go even for the few seconds it would take to undress and crawl into bed.

Carter gently kissed Tenny again and began to unbutton her blouse. Without letting her lips leave Tenny's, Carter explained, "Beds are for sex. Everywhere else is for love."

Chapter Twenty-one

The morning was already scorching and the air was so thick Tenny could taste it each time she swallowed. It tasted like it smelled, and she still had not discovered the reason for the fermentative odor of the air. Walking along the narrow wall which bordered the roadway, heading for Leblon, Tenny wanted to put some distance between herself and the hotel before she got a taxi. No curious cabbie was going to know where she was staying. Her mission this morning would most definitely pique the interest of any driver.

For the first time in years, in Carter's arms, Tenny slept through the night. Maybe the nightmares couldn't find her down here in this bewildering country. Tenny chuckled to herself. They were probably frightened to follow.

"Whoa." Tenny almost fell from the wall when a man suddenly stepped from the brush beside it. Fear filled her as she remembered all the warnings issued to tourists. She was trapped between the road which was busy with speeding morning commute traffic and the cliffs below. Sure that she had no other choice, Tenny stepped into a fighting stance, but kept her arms dangling at her side. The man seemed not to notice, brushed past Tenny and smiled. *"Bom dia."*

"Oh, good morning . . . I mean, *bom dia."* Tenny struggled to recall the greeting and even though she said it to his back, he turned and smiled at her again, appreciating her efforts. Tenny continued walking and admonished herself for making the poor guy feel like a felon. All the books had got her paranoid.

Reaching the southern end of Leblon beach, it was a short distance to a hotel where she would find plenty of taxis. She wanted to be careful. The assassin didn't know Carter would be traveling with her, and therefore Carter had registered them at the hotel. A killer would be watching for Tenny. But Rio was a huge city with two airports, dozens of hotels and millions of people. Tenny thought they would be relatively safe. He wouldn't bother to try and pick up her trail here. He would wait until they arrived at their destination, and by then she would be ready.

She ran up to the line of taxis and started asking each driver, *"Fala ingeles?"* She had memorized a few phrases from one of her tour books. None of the drivers would confess to knowing English if any did. So Tenny picked the smallest driver and jumped in the back of his cab. The size was only important if things went to shit. She wanted somebody she could control, just in case.

"Bom dia, quero ir para comprar un pistola." She

made a gun with her fingers as she finished her request. The man looked blankly at her. Tenny knew she had put the words together in a way that made sense, but she was unsure about the word for gun, which they didn't include in her tourist vocabulary list. She tried again. *"Quero ir para comprar un ..."* This time instead of using the word, she held up her hand again and made a gun, pointed at him, and said, "Bang, bang" as she mockingly shot him.

He shrugged and began to drive away from the hotel. Tenny was unsure if he had understood, but really had no choice but to wait and see. Sitting back she watched as they headed inland and then around the lake which sat in the middle of Rio. Now when she looked at Brazil she no longer felt intimidated by the unknown.

The driver started to slow and Tenny could see a beautiful bay out ahead of them. Then she looked up to her right and realized that they were at the base of Sugarloaf. The taxi came to a stop and the driver tapped at the meter, which Tenny noticed was not working. The driver shrugged again.

Tenny knew she wasn't going to like the answer, but asked anyway. *"Quanto eh?"*

"Forty thousand *cruzeiros.*" He said it fast in English.

"What! Are you nuts?" Tenny was trying to do the math quickly in her head, but it sounded outrageous.

"Forty thousand *cruzeiros!*" The small man was not so friendly this time.

Tenny started to pull worn *cruzeiros* away from the bundle she had received that morning at the exchange. Her poor math had indicated that it wasn't worth getting into an argument with this man. She handed him the money and asked, *"Onde e un pistola?"*

The driver grinned, gunned the engine, pointed to a building across the square and then sped away. Tenny knew people all right, and she instantly knew that he had taken advantage of a stupid American woman. The building he had pointed to had a formal entrance with huge letters above it announcing its proper title. Tenny wasn't sure what it all said, but she figured she knew what the word *militia* meant. A quick look around confirmed her suspicions. He had brought her to a military base, full of guns and soldiers.

"Perfect, I'll just walk up to one of these not-so-friendly looking policemen and ask for a gun." Tenny felt foolish as she looked around.

She started walking toward the entrance to the Sugarloaf tram, not knowing what else to do. A police car pulled alongside her and Tenny noticed that the officers inside had on different uniforms than the military police standing at the entrance to the square. She also noticed that the seal was two smoking revolvers with the barrels crossed. Tenny laughed as she thought, community policing must go over big down here.

With that type of symbol for the police, Tenny was expecting a real tough package to get out as the car came to stop in front of her and the officers exited. Once again Tenny couldn't help being amused. The officers wore no bullet-proof vests, no handcuffs, no baton, no portable radio, no chemical spray, only a pathetic two-inch, four-shot revolver. Suddenly Tenny felt safe in this country. How dangerous could it be if its officers were so poorly armed?

She turned and headed for the water. She had to get her head back on her mission. She needed a weapon. Preferably something with a little more firepower than what the police carried. Taking a seat on a bench along the far side of the square, Tenny began to watch the people, searching for a face she felt she could trust. She had to find a person who could help.

For a half an hour Tenny watched and waited. Then a taxi came up fast to the curb near the entrance to the trams. The driver jumped out and ran around to the other side to open the door and let the passengers out. The driver was all smiles.

Instantly Tenny was up and jogging toward the taxi. She had to catch it. Tenny had seen probably a hundred cabs come into the square, trade passengers and scoot away again. But they had all been the same. Tenny needed this taxi. It was special—the driver was a woman.

"Taxi!" Tenny sprinted the last few yards, as the woman was about to get back into her cab.

The woman driver looked up. "You want me or my car?" she teased.

Tenny missed the joke. "You speak English well."

The driver smiled. "Yours isn't bad either."

Relieved, Tenny returned her smile. The driver had the rich brown skin and black hair which made Tenny believe she was probably of Memelucos descent. But she spoke with an Australian accent, which confused Tenny.

"Where to, lady?"

"Corcovado." The statue was the only place Tenny knew by name, besides Sugarloaf.

"That is a good spot, very beautiful." The driver hadn't stopped smiling. She cranked the taxi into a tight turn, heading away from the square. "I am Vianna, and you?"

"Tenny."

"Tenny, what does that mean? I've never heard such a name." Vianna was glancing over her shoulder with a look of disbelief.

"Oh, well, my real name is Elizabeth. Tenny is only a nickname that my friends call me."

"Ah yes, you *Norte Americanos* like to do such things, no? It must make your mothers sad that you don't value your love-given name." Vianna was serious, and Tenny didn't know what to say. "I've been to New York and Los Angeles, they are nice, but not as special as Rio, no?" She paused.

"Well, I've never been to New York, but Rio is a beautiful city."

"Where do you live?"

"San Francisco." Easier than trying to explain where Bayview was located, Tenny figured.

"San Francisco is also a beautiful city. I've only seen pictures, but next time I come to your country I will visit San Francisco. I spent three years in Sydney, which is where I learned English. Then one in London. My mother got me positions as a nanny so that I could see more of the world than Brazil. This is important, no?" No pause, "But Brazil is the best. Our country has its problems, but all the others do also. So are you here for vacation?"

"No." Tenny needed to be honest. She needed help. "I'm here looking for my little girl. She was stolen from me and brought here."

The smile vanished from Vianna's face. "Why would somebody steal a child? It was her father, no?"

Tenny leaned over the front passenger seat. "No, it was a stranger who was paid to take her. Then she was sold to a couple living here in a city called Ouro Preto. I don't know why they did it. Brazil seems to have more children than it knows what to do with."

Vianna turned from the highway and found a place to pull to the side of the road. "You do not understand. In Brazil family means so much. It is not like the United States. Generations of families live under a single roof, that's how it's done. If you can provide for one more, then that's what you do. I myself am a child of the streets who my mother brought into her home as her own. But I am a part of her family for always."

Tenny had been referring to the homeless children that had made international news about four years ago when several were shot to death while they slept in the streets.

"The street children are viewed by many as a social

problem. They are mostly black and come from the rural areas. They gang together and cause crime."

Tenny did not want to anger the driver and kept her thoughts to herself. But she did want to understand. "Why didn't this couple just adopt a child from this country?"

"There aren't that many good children to have. Most are done informally, like myself."

Tenny was frustrated. "Well, why didn't they just go out and find a child from the streets then? Why did they have to destroy another family?"

Vianna seemed on the verge of tears. "I don't know why they did this. But street children aren't pure." Tenny swallowed a retort, then Vianna said, "What do you want of me?"

"I need your help." Tenny hesitated, unsure of how to continue without scaring this woman away. She couldn't afford to lose Vianna. "Look, the couple in the U.S. responsible for taking my child have sent a man to stop me from finding my little girl and he will kill me if he has to. I need a gun. I need you to help me find a gun."

Vianna sat back and exhaled. She ran her hands nervously through her short hair as she shook her head in disbelief. Tenny was sure that she had said too much too fast.

"I'll pay you well for your help."

Vianna furrowed her brows. For an instant, Tenny thought she had angered her only source of assistance. Then Vianna asked, "Who are you to carry a gun?"

"I used to be a police officer." Tenny watched Vianna's expression change as her eyes widened and she sucked in a small breath. Then she became instantly suspicious.

"You are the police?" But before Tenny could respond, she mumbled her own answer. "I remember seeing women police in North America. It is common, no?" She seemed intrigued.

173

"Yes, more and more women become officers each year." Tenny smiled with pride. "We're pretty good at it."

"Ah, but it is dangerous, so much violence in your country." Vianna still was somewhat awed.

"No more dangerous than a woman driving a taxi in Rio, no?" Tenny's indirect compliment brought a smile to Vianna's face.

She laughed. "Yes, sometimes I think I should carry my gun. But I drive mostly for my mother's clients and stay away from trouble. If I were caught with it by the *policia* it would be much more *perigosa*."

Tenny was excited. "Then you have a gun."

"Only for protection in my house, when I am alone." Vianna nodded.

"Then you can help me buy one."

"Yes, there are many guns. Easy to buy. But not safe for a woman." Vianna pulled the taxi back to the roadway. "Yes, I will help you, Tenny. I hope you have lots of money." Tenny sat back and smiled again. Vianna was a businesswoman also.

Chapter Twenty-two

Tenny leaned against the car while she watched Vianna's animated gestures as she spoke on the phone. Tenny wondered what she was saying, and to whom. The sun was merciless, forcing Tenny to look for shade, but the crowded commercial district didn't offer any shelter. She'd have to endure the heat.

After a while, Vianna hung up the phone and jogged back toward her cab. "My brother will get you what you need. He will have it for you tomorrow. Now I'll take you back to your hotel. I must get my mother's clients." She checked her watch as she yanked open the back door and darted around to the driver's side.

"Tomorrow is no good." Tenny lunged into the back

seat and touched Vianna's shoulder as she reached for the ignition key. "I must be on my way to Ouro Preto tomorrow. Every day is important. I need the gun today." Tenny had to get her to understand the urgency. Granted, Vianna had done well. What more could she expect? Tenny thought.

"You can have the gun by afternoon, catch a plane for Belo Horizonte and be in Ouro Preto by evening. It is my best." She turned and started the car. "Now I must get going."

Tenny was determined. "I can't wait. Take me to Rocinha. I'll find one myself." Tenny had read about this place. It was the world's largest shantytown and a center for drug trafficking. Tenny knew that where there were drugs, there were guns.

"*Socorro! Que legal!*" Vianna stomped on the brakes as she was pulling into traffic. Her abrupt stop was cursed by blaring horns. "You are *muito bonita*, all you will find is *perigo. Deixe-me em paz!* I take you back!" Vianna was clearly exasperated. Tenny wasn't sure what language she was speaking. "You are crazy."

Tenny leaned back and saw Vianna watching her in the rear view mirror. "I've already been told that," she said coolly.

"What of my mother's clients?"

Tenny relaxed, she was offering to help again. "I will make it worth your mother's inconvenience."

"This is a stupid thing," Vianna had been saying every few minutes since they had arrived.

The taxi was parked at the bottom of Rocinha as they formulated their plan before entering the *favela*. Tenny was practicing her phrases over and over, with occasional pronunciation corrections by Vianna. All she had time to learn was the Portuguese for "I need a gun and two clips. I will give you one hundred thousand *cruzeiros*."

"Don't say anything else. Nothing, do you understand?" Tenny nodded. "This is a stupid thing I'm letting you do. I will be responsible." Vianna seemed to be having second thoughts. Vianna looked her over. "You look like one of us, no? Give me those boots. You wear my shoes." She watched as Tenny removed her trendy hiking boots. "If they figure you for an *Norte Americano*, it won't be good." Tenny slid into Vianna's shoes while she gave Tenny one last look. "Give me the rest of your money." Vianna stuck her hand out. "I will hold it."

Tenny wondered if she was about to become the victim of an elaborate scheme to separate her from her cash. She handed Vianna the mix of *cruzeiros* and dollars. She had to trust her. There was no choice.

Vianna responded as if she had read Tenny's mind. "Don't worry. I will be there to get you out." She started the engine and moved the taxi up the narrow dirt road. "This is a stupid thing," she was muttering as she went.

Rocinha was a small city that stretched up the steep mountains behind the wealthy resort area of Sao Conrado. The dirt roads were uneven, the houses small brick boxes with roofs made from scrap material, and the people much darker than even Vianna. Many suspiciously eyed the taxi as it crept through the streets. Taxis did not come into the *favela*.

"I drop you here and pick you up here. You don't want them to see you coming in this car." Tenny understood as she got out. "Walk up that hill there." Vianna pointed to her left. "When you come to second cross street go right and look for the two-story building. Be careful!"

Tenny began walking up the hill at a casual pace. She reminded herself that she had been in ghettos before and this was a ghetto — nothing more, nothing less. She also reminded herself that people lived here because they were poor, not because they were bad. The danger was not from the people who watched her as she climbed the road, but from men who took advantage of this neighborhood, the criminals who chose to conduct their illegal activities among the poor because the poor wouldn't complain. Even if they did, who would listen? Not so different from home, Tenny thought.

She reached the second street and turned right. About one hundred yards away stood the two-story building. She started toward it. Her heart was racing, but she slowed her pace as if weary from the climb. She neared the entrance which, unlike many of the shacks, had a door. When she was within a few feet of the door a man stepped from the shadows. He had a short Afro which was greased back. His face was covered with a thick stubble which traveled unshaven down his neck. He was shirtless, not unusual in Rio, and his torso was marred by numerous scars. Tenny recognized one of the scars as a gunshot wound. She had the right place.

Tenny turned to ice, quelling all emotion. She made her request and purposely looked up and down the road as this doorman looked her up and down. He was not in charge, and she would not show him any respect. He would simply carry the message.

"*Espere.*" He disappeared into the building.

As she waited, Tenny watched an old woman come out of the shanty across the road. She stepped from the packed dirt floor to the dirt road. She was thin and frail, but her body wasn't bent by the age or the poverty. Her long hair, mixed to a sorrel, was tightly twisted and bound behind her head. She was carrying a small pan as if it were precious.

The tune the old woman hummed was mixed with meows and soon two cats appeared at her feet. She greeted them and set down the pan, then she briefly disappeared back inside. A box slid into the doorway and the old woman took a seat. In a bowl on her lap, she worked with some type of vegetable while she watched her friends gather.

Soon the road was full of cats. They had come from nowhere and everywhere. Each snatched a piece of food from the pan and scampered away, none trying to protect the pan for their own, sharing among themselves as the woman had done with them. The old woman was smiling.

"You wish a gun." The harsh deep voice surprised her. She spun back to the door but did not forget.

"*Que?*" Tenny shrugged at the man standing in the doorway.

He yelled, "You come here to buy gun?" It was an obvious attempt to get her to panic and give herself away. She did neither.

"*Nao falo ingeles.*" She hoped her accent was sufficient and didn't let her stare drift from his.

He was a large Mulatto with the muscles of an ex-con and tattoos on his arms and neck. He wore a clean, white T-shirt and khaki shorts with large pockets in which both hands were buried. Suddenly, Tenny felt quite at home. She had mad-dogged with the best assholes. This one was no different. After several minutes of this ritual, Tenny pulled out a bundle of *cruzeiros* and held it in front of her without taking her eyes from his.

He slowly looked down at the money and back to her. He brought a .45 caliber semi-automatic handgun from one of his pockets and held it by his side. Next, he slowly reached out and tried to take the money from Tenny's grasp. She would not let go. Challenged, he snapped the gun up into her face.

"You are not from here or else you would not be here." He spoke in English again.

Tenny had never had a gun inches from her face, but she remained calm. There was nothing else to do. "You must deal with my people often, your English isn't bad."

To try to continue her deception would imply that she thought him a fool. She didn't look at the gun; that would be a sign of weakness.

"No, none as stupid as you." He grabbed the barrel of the gun with his other hand and turned it toward her, offering the butt to Tenny while removing the money from her hand. A single magazine appeared from his other pocket and he handed it over also. Then he shut the door without another word. The deal was supposed to be for two magazines, but Tenny felt fortunate. She turned to leave and noticed that the cats were gone. The old woman was gone. Nobody was in sight. Nobody wanted to witness what should have taken place. Tenny felt more than fortunate, she felt lucky. When she noticed the taxi pass on a road below, she sprinted down after it.

Vianna must have seen her running toward the road, because before Tenny could reach the intersection, Vianna had reversed into it. Tenny thought about diving through the rear window which was rolled all the way down, but instead slowed just enough to yank open the door and jump in. "God, that was a stupid thing to do!"

Vianna pressed down hard on the accelerator and the car lurched forward and she spun it around the next corner, descending from Rocinha much too fast. Tenny didn't mind. She had seen enough of this part of Brazil.

Chapter Twenty-three

While Tenny had been busy getting the gun, Carter had been tending to more practical concerns. She had managed to get by with her high school Spanish and purchased two Varig air passes. She had also made arrangements to have a car meet them at the Belo Horizonte airport and transport them to Ouro Preto. When Tenny had returned from her adventure, Carter had the bags packed and was ready to go find her daughter.

Now as they approached Belo Horizonte, Carter stared out the window at the red earth which was so bright it gave the impression that it was toxic. The rich earth not only hosted treasures within its soil, it gave life to green hillsides and thick forests. Just another bizarre reality in this complicated country.

Carter glanced back at Tenny, who was studying the page of her guidebook. Carter understood Tenny's need to know it all, to be prepared. It had always been Tenny's obsession and it was what made her different from all the rest. She was never satisfied. It was this passion that would always keep them apart.

"How are we going to find them? We don't have an address." Carter was becoming apprehensive as they neared Ouro Preto.

"Well, we have the name, we'll ask around until somebody can tell us where Joao Sousa lives." Tenny tried to sound nonchalant to reduce Carter's anxiety.

"Joao, good man." The driver spoke with a thick Brazilian accent and it took both Tenny and Carter a moment to realize what he had said.

Shaking from excitement, Tenny leaned forward in the back seat. She tried to sound calm. "You know Joao?"

"*E*, good man."

"He's a friend of a friend and I'm suppose to look him up while we're in Ouro Preto. Can you tell me where he lives?" Tenny forgot the language barrier in her excitement.

The driver gave her a shrug and said, "*Nao*."

"You don't know where he lives." Coolness crept into her voice.

Again only a shrug.

Carter grabbed Tenny and pulled her back and then she leaned forward. "*Fala ingles*?"

"*Nao*."

"*Fala Español*?"

"*Picito,*" he said in Spanish.

"*Donde viva Joao Sousa?*" Carter asked as Tenny searched the Brazilian glossary in her book.

"*En la casa,*" the driver said as if everybody knew.

Carter was fighting frustration. "I know he lives in a house, but *donde? Que calle?*"

"*No se. Señor Sousa viva en la casa.*"

"The house." Tenny shook her head, disappointed. "Great, we know he lives in the house."

Carter persisted. "*Tu tamar me va la casa.*"

"*E.*"

Carter sat back and Tenny asked, "What did he say yes to?"

"I think I asked him to take me to the house."

"What do you mean, you think? You don't know what you asked?" Tenny was abrupt.

"Look, Tenny, I did my best. I think he got the point." Carter met Tenny's impatience with calm. "I guess we'll find out soon though." She pointed out the windshield as Ouro Preto suddenly came into view.

The sun escaped from the clouds at the same moment, spotlighting the town for its visitors. At first all they saw were buildings riding the crests of the rolling hills which were tucked down beneath the clouds which hung to the mountains surrounding the town. Hundreds of clean white walls met the rust red of tiled roofs. As they drew closer, they began to pick out the dramatic churches which occupied each of the town's small peaks.

Tenny and Carter forgot about the house as the car entered the narrow stone streets of Ouro Preto. Neither had ever seen anything like this town. The buildings crowded the narrow streets that allowed passage of only a single vehicle. Each building had rows of windows, half of which were occupied by people simply watching the passersby. Tourists and locals strolled along the soapstone slab sidewalk but nobody seemed in a hurry. Urgency was clearly not a part of life in this historic town, which was in no rush to move into the future.

They passed through the town's principal plaza and the driver announced, *"Praca Triadentes"* as he slowed down a steep passage to another ridge. Then, before maneuvering down to another, lower hill, he stopped and pointed. *"La Casa."*

Tenny smiled. No wonder they called it "the house." In this town where every available space had been crammed with structures, this house stood alone. Surrounded by thick foliage and tall trees, only the front of the house was visible as it faced out to the town from its perch. The nearest building was over thirty yards away.

The driver continued down the road as Tenny turned to look out the back window. She was thinking that the Sousa family was obviously special, and that worried her. She had no idea what Carter was thinking, but they watched the house until it was blocked from view. Tenny imagined that she had been watching for her baby. They were close.

"Let's go." Carter set her bag down and headed back out of the room.

"Whoa, hold on." Tenny barely managed to grab her arm. "We're not going anywhere. You don't think we're simply going to march up to Señor Sousa's house and demand your child back?"

Carter looked at Tenny as if she had become part of the enemy camp. "My baby's in that house and I'm here to get her back." She tried to pull away. "Let me go. What's wrong with you? I want my baby." Carter was struggling, the tears were rushing from her eyes.

Tenny kept a tight hold on Carter and shut the door,

not wanting to share their intentions with the entire *pousada*. Tenny dragged her to a bed and pulled her down beside her. "Look, we can't do it like that for several reasons. First, you saw the house. This family is not like the rest of the people who live here. That house is like a palace here. The Sousas must be important people. We need to be careful."

Tenny relaxed her grip and Carter ripped herself free and vaulted to her feet. "This is not a time to go slow and careful, Tenny. Damn it, my little girl is in that house and I intend to go get her, with or without your help."

Tenny lunged to block her access to the door and once again the space between them was charged with emotion— this time, it was anger.

"Damn it, we don't know what Jenkins told these people. He didn't know that I was going to find them this quick. He couldn't have known. But the Jenkinses are not stupid and they cover all their tracks. And that's the second reason we're not going to go rush over there and demand that they return Kelsey." Tenny tried gently to lead Carter from the door, but she would not budge. Tenny continued in a softer, but still serious voice. "There's an assassin out there somewhere and he's waiting for us to be careless."

Carter's shoulders relaxed somewhat and her defiant stare slipped to the floor. When she looked up again, fear had devoured her rage. Her voice trembled. "What are you talking about?"

"The Jenkinses hired somebody to stop us from finding Kelsey. When Caroline scanned the call from Jenkins to Sousa, she also intercepted another call from Jenkins. It was to a man whose instructions are to make sure we don't find Kelsey alive." Tenny reached out and took Carter's hand, but Carter stiffened. "Kelsey is the only evidence of their crimes that's vulnerable to exposure. Jenkins doesn't want to hurt his business by killing customers, but if it's the only option left, that's what he'll do. That's why we have to go slow. We have to be careful, for Kelsey's sake."

Carter said, "I'm going to get my daughter back."

"I know, but we're going to do it my way." Tenny yanked her bag from the floor and started to dig through it. "First, let's try to find some stuff to wear that doesn't look so *Norte Americano*, eh? These shirts with logos are out and so are the jean shorts." Carter was already searching her own clothing. "Then we'll go have a closer look at *la casa*." Tenny explained her plan.

Carter passed again by the iron gates set in the tall stone wall which bordered the sidewalk. A disinterested glance revealed an overgrown stone driveway which twisted downward, divulging nothing of *la casa*. Tenny had been right. This house was special. Once a person got close to it, it magically disappeared into the Brazilian hillside. The trees and bushes completely blocked it from view. Carter had tried the street above and below it, but neither had provided her with a chance to get the information she had been sent to gather.

Carter kept walking and approached an alley which she knew must pass by the house. She checked the landmarks she had used to first establish the house's location. The alley should descend down the hill, she thought, passing by her target. Yet the alley frightened her. She had already passed it once, too intimidated to enter. It was steep and even narrower than the streets, lined with high walls. The twisting alley was overgrown and dirty. It did not look like a place for her to explore.

Carter wondered where Tenny was. Would Tenny want her to travel down what appeared to be a perilous alley? Cursing, she drew closer to the entrance. Tenny was too good at this stuff. Carter hadn't seen her since they both left the *pousada*. She hoped she hadn't lost Tenny, but then laughed at herself for even thinking that she could lose that woman. She made up her mind, ducking into the alley, confident that she'd be safe. Tenacity was watching.

"Shit! No! Not the alley!" Tenny muttered as she watched Carter from a small store down the street. The man behind the counter looked at her, unsure of what had suddenly displeased his customer.

Tenny fought the urge to sprint after Carter, even though there was no way to protect her in the alley. She reminded herself that Carter had been doing an excellent job of blending into her environment. Casually strolling and smiling. Welcoming others in their native tongue. Not appearing to be doing anything unusual. Tenny had not noticed anybody watching her. Plus, now would be her best chance to see if somebody else was indeed following her. They would have to enter the same alley, which wasn't heavily traveled. Carter had the been the first to enter or exit it since Tenny had been watching.

Tenny casually purchased some candy as she continued to watch. Nobody followed. But what if Carter didn't know to come back out the way she went in? What if there was another side entrance to the alley?

Tenny charged from the store and across the street, sacrificing anonymity, sure now that she had made a terrible mistake by letting Carter take this risk. At the alley's entrance, she did not see Carter anywhere along the treacherous path. She started down the corroding steps. Wanting to draw her weapon and be ready, Tenny resisted her training, not wanting to attract any more attention than she already had. As she approached another corner in the alley, she saw a woman standing in a window of a small shack on the left side. The woman had her back to Tenny as she watched something farther down and around the corner.

Tenny rounded the curve and saw who was holding the woman's attention. Carter was trying to hoist herself up the side of the stone wall which bordered the right side of the alley. Unsuccessful in her efforts, Carter tried to open a wooden gate built into the wall. The Sousas definitely liked their privacy, which their neighbor probably understood. Carter was hardly being discreet.

Tenny slowed to a casual pace and approached Carter. She wanted to admonish her for her carelessness, but Tenny knew that speaking would expose them as strangers to this country and this alley. They were being watched. Instead, she decided to teach Carter a lesson and crept up directly behind Carter, as the rookie spy tried to peek through a hole in the gate. As she passed, Tenny coughed loudly. Carter jumped back from the gate and lost her footing on the uneven paving stones. She fell to the ground in surprise. Tenny didn't even pause to see if Carter was all right.

Chapter Twenty-four

There was a break in the rain. It had been pouring off and on since evening. When they had returned from their scouting mission the day before, Tenny had decided it would be best for them to lie low until the darkness could provide protection, then she would return to the house. They had rested the best they could today, and now Tenny was dressed in dark clothing, but not too dark. Brazilians seemed to never sleep, and Tenny would attract attention strolling through town dressed all in black. She stood to leave.

"They're there, aren't they?" Carter said.

"All I know, babe, is that Jenkins called to warn the

Sousas. There's no way of telling how they reacted." She didn't want to raise Carter's hopes.

Carter stared down at her hands clenched in her lap. "If it were me, I'd run like hell."

"I'll be back. Be ready." For anything, she silently added.

The next storm was moving in fast with swirling gusts that rushed through the streets. The severe weather helped to move people off the streets and back from their window perches. Tenny quickly located a place in the wall along the alley where no curious eyes could watch. She clambered over the wall, thankful that crime in Ouro Preto apparently wasn't bad, since this wall did not have the broken glass shards on top that the walls of Rio did.

She landed among the dense, green growth and started to move in the direction of the house. Her pace through the jungle of a yard was slow due to the darkness which seemed untouched by Tenny's small penlight. The claustrophobic overgrowth exaggerated the sound of her heartbeat. Maybe the darkness had not been a good idea. For some reason, she felt like she was at a disadvantage and snapped off the light. If the darkness was going to be her ally, she would have to work within it, otherwise it would be her enemy. She stopped to listen for any sounds which would indicate that she was not alone. There were none, and eventually the house came into view.

It was a brilliant white with maroon and blue trim. The roof was steeply pitched and the water from the storm still trickled over the edges. A large balcony on the second floor no doubt provided a view of several churches; the only other structures in this town which enjoyed open space. It was a beautiful house with a feeling of warmth. But Tenny noticed that each of the windows was dark.

There was no indication of life within. As Tenny crept forward, she knew that her search would not end tonight.

The heavy wooden doors were securely bolted, but the windows were not so stubborn. One was particularly loose in its frame, and with a little persuasion it slipped easily upward. In less than a week, this was the second home Tenny had illegally entered. What am I doing? she asked herself as she crawled through the window.

Once inside, Tenny immediately knew that Kelsey was gone. All the furniture was covered, closets stood open and empty, ashes of burned paper littered the fireplace. Tenny checked the entire house simply as an exercise in thoroughness, but found nothing. That same numbness was spreading through her body again as she started toward the window. She forced herself to continue, uncertain if she would ever be one step ahead instead of two behind.

Suddenly the house exploded with a drumming force that sent Tenny to the floor as she sought cover. In a moment, when Tenny's heart began to slow again, she realized that the sound was only the rain which had finally begun to spill again over this town. It was as loud as hail, but of course, in the humid climate it was typical. Tenny would be soaked the moment she stepped from *la casa*.

She trotted down the garden path which led to the wall-gate in the alley. By the time she reached the alley, it had already turned into a small stream, the water sweeping past. Tenny was glad she had picked her hiking boots for tonight's intrusion. The footing in the alley having already become impossible, she slipped several times as she negotiated her way down the seldom traveled passage. Toward the bottom, the flat street lay only feet away and Tenny let herself go. Momentum brought her to a run, as she and the water emptied out onto the street below.

She glimpsed a person to her right as she exited the alley and instantly Tenny's mind warned her of the danger. She struggled to analyze what she'd seen while her body already was reacting. Turning, she threw herself into a doorway only feet away. The bullet crashed against the red bricks as her body collided with the door. The impact knocked the picture of what she had seen back to her mind. It was him. There was no doubt. There were no blonds in this town.

Quickly she ducked from the doorway and zigzagged about thirty yards to a long path of steps which led to another street below. There was no sound, but she knew he was still firing, the silencer he used effectively protecting him from being discovered. Tenny didn't bother to draw her own weapon; its discharge would not be quieted or confused for thunder. A confrontation with the Brazilian authorities would also end her search. She was not prepared to give up—not yet. She would only use the gun if it was a life or death situation.

Tenny glanced back up the street before darting down the stairs and saw the figure pursuing her through the rain. Within the first ten steps Tenny lost her footing in the rushing water and fell to the ground. Tumbling down the long, straight, bone-crushing stairs, Tenny knew she had no cover and no escape. She could only hope that he didn't stop to think before he followed down the punishing path.

The crumbling stones of the stairs disintegrated each time Tenny tried to reach out and end her disastrous descent. Sliding, twisting, bouncing, rolling, she wasn't sure she would survive the fall. Everything else was tossed from her mind as she landed on her back, with the gun in the small of her back caving into her spine. The pain was tremendous. But she was still falling, out of control, with no time to consider the agony of one blow before the next was upon her. Finally she flew off the stairs and into a wall, ending her plummet.

She attempted to stand, but her body was slow to

respond. She had only tumbled down about thirty steps, halfway from the bottom. Expecting the bullets to start ripping into her at any moment, Tenny turned back toward the top of the steps and drew her gun. But no confrontation would be necessary, as she recognized the figure rushing toward her like a reckless boulder. He had not been too smart in his pursuit. Now his heavier weight was carrying him past her with neck-breaking momentum.

Tenny flattened herself against the wall to avoid being struck by the man bearing down upon her. Then, as he passed harmlessly, she jerked herself to her feet, scrambled back up the stairs and disappeared into the rain-soaked darkness.

Tenny peeked into the *pousada* before entering. The electricity was apparently out; the entire inn was eerily dark with small candles scattered about the rooms. Tenny grabbed a candle from the unattended front desk and began her ascent of the dark, narrow, steep stairway. Tenny cursed. She was really starting to hate stairs.

Carter rushed from the other room as she heard Tenny enter. "Well, what did you find?" When she caught sight of Tenny, horror rushed into Carter's face. "My God! Oh God, are you all right? Oh shit! Sit down." Carter helped her to the couch.

Tenny put a hand to the back of her head. She could feel a large gash and the sticky blood matting her hair. Her hands were bruised and swollen. Each movement was agonizing.

Carter disappeared and returned with a warm, damp washcloth. She began to dab at Tenny's head.

"Ouch! That hurts." Tenny whined. She examined her bloodied hands. "Oh shit, I'm still bleeding. I hate blood."

"Come on, let's get into the bathroom and try to clean you up some." Carter was already pulling Tenny to her feet against her groaning protest. "Is Kelsey safe? Was she there?"

"The house was empty. They're gone and I met our friend, Mr. Assassin. But round one goes to Miss Tenacity. We're not out of this fight yet. We'll find her."

Chapter Twenty-five

The darkness seemed to be closing in on her. If she had been at home, she would have just crawled out of bed, headed for her mother's room and found the comfort which even the danger of the dark could not intimidate. But she was not at home and her mother was not in the room across the hall.

She looked up at the ceiling, hoping her mother was watching from heaven. "Mommy, I don't know what to do. They want me to stay here and be their little girl, but you always told me that Elizabeth would take care of me. But she's not here and you're gone. They said you're dead. You and Daddy, but I never got to see you buried. I thought dead people got buried, why wouldn't I see you buried?" Kelsey's mind started to create a graveyard in the darkness. Tombstones were sprouting from the emptiness all over the room. Her fear was uncontrollable. "Why did that man take me? Why am I here? Mommy!" The ghosts were upon her, "Mommy help! Help me!"

Tenny twisted awake and the memories of the night before jolted her, pain accentuating her every movement. For a moment she hesitated opening her eyes, wondering if that too would hurt. When she did, the grayness of early morning greeted her. Slowly she scanned the room.

Carter was leaning against the wall, staring out into the streets of Ouro Preto. One hand was shoved deep into her pants pocket. In her other hand she held the gun.

Carter hated guns. She had always refused to allow Tenny to bring one into their home. She had never touched one before. The idea of using one was barbaric to her. Now, she stood silently, clutching the weapon.

"What are you doing, babe?" Tenny whispered through the silence.

She didn't respond. Nothing said, no movement, not even a blink of the eye — only stillness. Tenny eased herself to her feet, ignoring her pain, and moved to Carter's side. She reached down and took the weight from Carter's hand.

Tenny set the gun down on the bed and then moved in behind Carter. She wrapped her arms around Carter's thin waist and held her tight. There was nothing she could do to chase the demons from Carter's tortured mind. Tenny would have cried if there had been any tears left to shed.

After a while, Carter folded her arms across Tenny's. "I want my baby back, but I'm frightened that I might lose you too."

Tenny leaned her head against Carter's. "You're not going to lose me."

"I can't believe that for all the time we were together and you were a cop, I never worried about losing you." Carter shook her head in disbelief. "I guess I just never let myself think about it. Now, I feel as if I have to choose between you and my daughter. I can't —"

"You don't have to choose. I'm going to get Kelsey back and we're *all* going to go home. I promise you." Tenny hated making another promise.

Carter swiveled to face her, and Tenny flinched with the movement. "Look at you. How can you even manage to stand?"

"I'm not, you're holding me up." Tenny smiled encouragingly. "Let's get to work. We need to find somebody who knows where the Sousas went."

"What about our friend?" Carter glanced back out the window, as if he was waiting in the street below.

"There are too many people around during the day. We'll make sure we don't wander away from the crowd. He won't try anything when there's a good chance of him getting caught. He wants to go home too." Tenny refused to sound worried.

"Won't he find us, though?"

"Sure, probably soon after we step from this room. But he'll only watch us and I'll watch him." Tenny made it all sound so routine. "Of course, if we're lucky, he broke something important on those damn stairs last night and is out of commission." Tenny didn't think that it was a far-fetched possibility. She started to try to dress herself.

A hat concealed the gash in her head. Sunglasses hid most of the bruises and cuts on her face. Long pants and a light rain jacket covered the rest of the evidence of

Tenny's encounter. The gun was shoved into the front of her pants, the small of her back being much too tender to host the weapon today. They had agreed that Tenny would keep a low profile while Carter did all the talking. Once again, Tenny's main responsibility would be to watch and protect.

Exiting another store, Carter glanced at Tenny who sat at the base of the statue in the center of the main plaza. Tenny was scanning the faces of day and didn't see her. Carter entered the next store.

"Oh, my God."

For a brief moment Carter had thought she had found tomorrow. The girl seated behind the counter looked so much like Kelsey. But it was only another cruel deception. The little girl was about Kelsey's age and had her same soft brown hair and inquisitive brown eyes. She was even humming a song that was one of Kelsey's favorites. Carter couldn't stand to look at this child and turned to leave without seeking any answers. Nobody knew where the Sousas were anyway. Why would this child be any different?

Carter was out the door before the thought struck her. That song was her favorite Grateful Dead song. She had taught it to Kelsey. How would a child in Brazil know that song? It was far from the top forty tunes that found their way to Brazilian radio.

Rushing back into the store, Carter thrust the flier she had brought with her at the child, interrupting her song. "*Su amiga?*" She struggled to recall her Spanish while the adrenaline careened through her body.

The little girl looked at Carter strangely. Not as if she was frightened by Carter's emotional plea, but rather, confused by the words hurled at her. She said nothing. In the commotion, an elderly woman emerged from behind a curtain. She looked annoyed.

Carter tried to explain. "I don't mean to be rude. I'm

198

looking for my little girl." She pointed to the picture as she held up the flier. Now the woman looked confused too.

"You speak English?" The woman managed to say well enough for Carter to understand.

"Yes, yes. Do you?"

The woman spoke to the little girl in Portuguese. The girl jumped down from her stool and was out the door before Carter could understand what was happening.

"No, please don't go. Please! I need to ask you something." Carter started after her.

"*Nao*, come wait," the woman said to Carter.

The child was gone.

The quick movement from the store captured Tenny's attention. The little girl ran from the store, past Tenny and up the hill out of the plaza.

"Shit." Tenny moved toward the store as quickly as she could without drawing attention or further injuring her broken body. What was it now? What was the child running from?

Standing to one side of the storefront window, she watched for several moments before entering. What was going on? Carter was standing at the counter frantically gesturing at a woman who was patiently ignoring her and presenting souvenir after souvenir to Carter. Obviously, Carter had slipped and been identified as a North American. Now the woman was trying to pry the U.S. dollars from this stubborn tourist.

Stepping inside the store, Tenny inquired, "What's going on?"

"They know something, I'm sure. The girl was singing our song. She has to know." Carter's desperation crammed her words together so quickly that Tenny only got about half of them.

Carter would not relinquish her position at the counter which she seemed to think would somehow prevent the escape of this old woman.

Tenny stepped beside Carter. "Hey, slow down and tell me what's going on."

"I'd like to know that too." His voice was deep, his English perfect. Tenny and Carter spun to see the little girl with a young man in hand.

But before either could speak, the woman began to chatter in Portuguese as she came around the corner of the counter. She removed the flier from Carter's hand, passing it to the man. He studied it silently. Finally, he looked up from the announcement of iniquity.

"This is your child?" he asked, handing the flier back to Carter.

"Yes, and she was here with the Sousa family."

"How do you know that?" He sounded defensive.

Tenny took over. "My name is Elizabeth Mendoza and I was hired by the girl's mother to find her. I've been working with the FBI and local authorities, who tracked the child to Ouro Preto and the Sousas." Normally it was easy to casually intimidate people into cooperation by making everything sound officious. She hoped her small lies would do the trick—they didn't.

"If you're working with the FBI, why aren't they down here, and why haven't the Brazilian authorities been made aware of this?"

Tenny quickly debated. He held their answers. She couldn't risk the wrong approach. "Look, the truth is that nobody knows we're here. Nobody knows she's here." Tenny pointed at Kelsey's image on the flier. "Nobody back in the good old U.S.A. wants to even admit that child abduction is a problem." Tenny suddenly became angered by the thought of all the other children still out there, those still waiting to disappear. She snatched the flier out

200

of Carter's hands. "And this is a child we need to find. She can lead us to others."

The young man was tall and had a beaked nose and ears that stood out from his head. A permanent ring in his hair meant he usually wore a hat. The joints of his body were sharp with jutting bones. He placed his hands on his hips.

"I'm a guest in this country, just like the two of you." He nodded at them. "I'm only a student here at the university. The Sousas are very important people. This town worships them. When that little girl came into their lives the entire town celebrated for the continuance of that family. Do you understand?"

Tenny stared at him and let all the anger drain from her body. "You're protecting child-stealers. They destroyed her family" — Tenny didn't have to point to Carter — "to make their own. Do you understand?"

He shrank before her stare, yet he offered nothing. The woman poked at his ribs and questioned him. He explained in Portuguese and she looked to Carter. Without a word she took Carter into her arms and held her as if she were her own daughter. The woman looked back at the man and chastised him.

"She thinks you have the features of your daughter and knows that you are telling the truth. She would like to apologize for her friends the Sousas, and explains that the curse of their family must have finally been too much. Why else would somebody do such a terrible thing?" He paused as the woman interrupted once more. "She says nobody may destroy a family." He moved past Tenny, toward the counter. "Let me write down where you can find them."

Chapter Twenty-six

They both stared out the windows of the taxi as it maneuvered through the aging, poverty-stricken city of Salvador. The faces of the people here contained no hope, no determination, no anger.

The taxi pulled into the driveway of the hotel and the driver tapped the meter. "Sixteen thousand *cruzeiros*."

Steve fingered his wad of Brazilian currency, and Ashley removed three bills which she handed to the driver. She allowed Steve to gather their baggage. No bellboys rushed forward to assist.

When Tenny called from the Chicago Airport, she had only had time to tell them her destination. After a few days of hearing nothing from her, Steve and Ashley became concerned. Tenny had a way of taking on more than others would attempt, although she always seemed to manage. Something told them that this time would be different.

Nothing about this investigation had been simple, yet the relative ease in which the pieces had come together could create that misperception. Tenny kept rushing further and further into the unknown and away from those that could help. The people involved in this child-stealing operation would not let their profitable business end so easily. Tenny would need help and they intended to be there when she did.

It had not taken much convincing to get Caroline to tell them everything. She had come to the same conclusion — Tenny could not end this alone. But her opinion wasn't based on instinct. Caroline knew the facts. Her sources, which seemed endless, revealed that the Sousas were on the move. They were scared, not of Tenny, but of what the Jenkinses might do next. Caroline was sure that Tenny would not be able to find them in that huge country. She wasn't even certain that they were still in Brazil. This family had the financial ability to go international in their game of hide and seek. Caroline had no doubt that Tenny and Carter were in danger.

Caroline had also discovered that the Sousas had property along the coast, north of Salvador. This information had been extremely difficult to obtain. She didn't think that Tenny would be able to obtain it, and she told Steve and Ashley to start looking for Tenny in Ouro Preto.

Steve and Ashley knew Tenny better. They would find Kelsey. Wherever she was, Tenny would eventually appear, like a ghost searching for its lost soul so that it could finally rest. She would materialize and they would be waiting.

"I wonder what it's been like for the two of them." Ashley was lying on the bed, trying to forget about the heat by distracting her mind with other thoughts.

"What are you talking about?" Steve was standing at the open window waiting for even a small breeze.

"Carter and Tenny, you know, being back together. Aren't you curious?"

"No. Anyway, it's not her that has prevented Tenny from falling in love, it's Tenny. She won't allow herself to fall in love with anybody else because she could lose. She simply doesn't want to lose anymore." Steve's logic annoyed his partner who preferred her romantic visions.

"Said like a true man, taking all the emotion out of the situation. Maybe Tenny believes that every person can only have one true love. Maybe Carter was her true love."

Steve laughed sarcastically and turned to face Ashley, but he didn't move from the window, still waiting for coolness. "I can't believe we just submitted a leave of absence request and left. You're supposed to wait until they're approved. We may as well have quit!" Steve grabbed his head. "I can't believe I just emptied my bank account. I can't believe that we're down here in fucking Brazil, melting in this damn heat, looking for some killer, looking for Tenny, looking for an abducted child — and you want to speculate about Tenny's fucking love life!" Steve shook his head. "In case you were in dreamland, we have no guns, badges or authority. That thing called a passport we had to present at the airport means that we're in someone else's fucking world and nobody here gives a shit if we make it back to our own world or not." Steve's voice was rising. "How exactly do you think we're going to be able to help, even when we do find her? We're as good as helpless ourselves."

Ashley sat up. "You think badges are the only thing that gives us power?"

"I know, I know," Steve said guiltily.

"We'll be together again. We make an impressive team." Ashley shrugged. "Then we'll find a way to get Kelsey back." Ashley spoke casually, confidently. "Besides, when we solve this case they'll be begging us to come back to Los Palos P.D."

"Shit, every day you just become more and more like her."

"Thanks." Ashley smiled.

Chapter Twenty-seven

"I'll go check the house out this afternoon while you make arrangements to get us out of the country." Tenny was sitting at a poolside table, writing out all the different tactics they might use to get Kelsey back. It always helped her to think when she wrote things down. It required much more detailed and careful thought in order to put an idea on paper. "Don't forget that you need to get Kelsey a ticket. Shit! How are we going to get her out without a passport? Damn, we're going to have to get her papers or whatever they have for her. Great! I can just see it now, 'Excuse me we're stealing our child back and oh, by the way, can you please give us her papers too?' Perfect, just perfect!"

Tenny noticed that Carter didn't seem worried. In fact, Carter didn't seem to be listening at all. She was looking over the balcony, down to the busy, crowded streets. Tenny knew the expression on her face. It was pure fascination. Something had captured her attention.

"What is it?" Tenny stood and moved next to Carter.

"That child is incredible." She pointed at a skinny black boy who looked like he was about eight years old. "Watch him. He's got this little business going on with the cleaners there. He'll run the clothes back and forth from customers that pull up in their cars so they won't have to worry about parking. Plus, I've watched . him run about four other errands for people who drive up. Then, when he's not busy with that, he solicits tourists or obvious foreigners." Carter crossed her arms, which she always did when she was on the verge of tears, as if to hold back her emotions. "He's so young and he works harder than most adults I know."

Carter hadn't been exaggerating, Tenny noted. This kid was really hustling. No free moment was used to rest or to count his earnings or to play with the other kids on the streets. He was working.

After a few minutes, Tenny sat down again, bored. She really didn't see whatever it was that fascinated Carter. This was a poor country. Salvador was a poor city. He was a poor boy. He had to work. Anyway, she had more important things to think about and so did Carter.

"Did you hear what I said a few minutes ago?" Tenny was somewhat annoyed.

"Yes."

"Aren't you worried? Don't you want to talk about how we're going to get her?" She didn't understand Carter's latest mood. In Ouro Preto she had been so determined, practical and prepared to face anything. Now she seemed like the same old Carter, taking life one day at a time, making the most of each and every minute, no matter what the circumstances.

She sat down next to Tenny. "I don't know how to explain it, but no, I'm not worried." Her eyes were piercing. "When that wonderful woman hugged me in Ouro Preto and spoke about family, I knew that mine would be okay." Carter took Tenny's hands and squeezed them as if trying to transfer her confidence. "For the first time since this whole nightmare began, I really felt like things were going to be okay. I keep having flashes of it being over and us flying home together. I know that this time we're really going to find her."

Tenny said nothing, let go of Carter's hands and walked away from the table. Her anger gave her no choice but to retreat or attack. She didn't see it as Carter trying to share her confidence. Instead, it was as if Carter was releasing all the responsibility. Once again, the whole burden for making things right fell upon Tenny. She didn't want it. She was tired, hurt, unsure, and she was frightened. She needed to walk, to think.

The hard-working boy rushed up to her and asked her something in a language she didn't recognize. Tenny kept walking and he stuck to her hip as he switched to another language. Tenny sped up to discourage his efforts. He trotted beside her and tried yet another language. She stopped abruptly and it took him several steps to brake himself, but he was already trying his fourth language.

"How many ways can you ask?" Tenny couldn't help but smile. The kid was persistent.

"American? You are American? You don't look like an American."

Tenny was so perturbed, she nearly missed the fact that he spoke almost perfect English. "What does that mean? What the hell do think you Americans look like?" She eyed him closely. "Hey, how do you know English?"

"Before my mother died she told me that communication would be the key to my success. She planned great things for me. I learn any language that I need and don't already know." He was not shy. "Last year I learn English while helping a student. She left me books and a dictionary so that I could continue. You give me a book that tells me how, and I can learn anything."

Tenny didn't doubt him for a moment. She liked this kid; he reminded her of Angelica. Suddenly, Tenny felt a dull sensation at the base of her neck. The uncomfortable feeling spread quickly to her shoulders. Somebody was watching her.

Instinctively, Tenny knew which way to turn to catch the visual intruder. Carter smiled and waved from the balcony. She had known this boy was special without even talking to him. Tenny wondered how.

"So can I help?" The boy would not give up.

"Help with what?" Tenny turned back to him.

"Help you and your friend." He waved to Carter and she waved back.

Tenny had an odd feeling, as if these two operated in another dimension. It was so strange, she had to explore further. "What makes you think that we need help?"

"Because she is lost. I can help." He didn't indicate a specific person.

Tenny thought she was beginning to understand what Carter had tried to tell her earlier — this kid was different. She wondered if somehow he really knew, or if he was simply so good at communicating that he could say the right thing; maybe he just knew the correct words to use, without understanding their meaning.

At the moment, though, she really didn't care. He could help. "Here, go get us a car and be back in half an hour." She handed him a bunch of dollars.

"This is a fortune to me. What makes you think I'll be back?" He looked at her as if she was crazy to have faith in him.

"Because great men can be trusted." Tenny walked away.

He handed most of the money back to Tenny. "I got a good deal and took a small commission for myself."

She ignored his gesture. "Keep it. You're not done yet. Get in." Tenny climbed in behind the wheel as the boy ran around to the other side of the car without hesitation. He jumped in next to her, smiling with expectation, the type of smile that only children possessed. Tenny couldn't resist laughing, it had been so long.

Once he had helped her to negotiate the city traffic, introduced her to the Brazilian style of driving — "if there is no crash, then it is all right" — and directed her to the highway, Tenny could concentrate less on her driving and more on her passenger.

"What's your name?"

"Jorge. My mother named me after a famous Brazilian author. She always said that he had a special way of communicating and I needed to learn it, then take it one step further."

"What's your name?"

"Elizabeth, but my friends call me Tenny, short for Tenacity."

"I don't know this word, *tenacity*?"

Tenny laughed — finally something this kid didn't know. "It means I have a hard head."

"Ah, you mean stubborn."

"Something like that." She needed to tell him what was going on. She knew he could help, but not without knowing their mission. "So how much English do you know?"

"English is my best language. My mother said it would take me the furthest. It is spoken around the world. Japanese is my second best language. It is very difficult to learn, though. I had to move to São Paulo for two years so that I could learn. The Japanese are a special people. It is an important language to know." He rattled off several sentences in what sounded to her like Japanese. Then he sat back, pleased.

Tenny was amazed. "How old are you?"

Jorge looked as if he was insulted by the question. "I'm small for my age in size, but not inside." He tapped his head. "I am twelve."

"Well, Jorge, let me assure you, when I speak with you it is as if I'm talking with an adult." She could tell that this pleased him even more. The smile was back. "Let me tell you exactly what we're doing and what we're facing. You can ask me to let you out of this car at any time and you can keep the money." Tenny launched into her story as they sped north along the coast.

"Pull off here. That's it there across the water." Jorge was out of the car before it even came to a complete stop. "Open the hood," he commanded as he pounded it once. Tenny unlatched it and Jorge stood it up. Then he took a plastic container of water from his pack and carefully

211

spilled some across the engine — instant steam. Next he dramatically walked around to the side of the car and kicked the tire. "Stupid car!"

Jorge flung himself down to the sandy, soft dirt. He squinted at the house which stood alone across the bay. Tenny joined him, uncomfortable with being out in the open. The assassin knew what she looked like, and she doubted Jorge's little ploy would fool him.

The Sousas had a passion for dramatic homes. This one was no less prestigious than the one in Ouro Preto. It also stood by itself with the nearest house about seventy-five yards away. It backed up to a tall, glistening white sand dune planted with scattered shrubbery. Only the dark, tinted windows broke the whiteness of the scene. Nearby, the bay greeted the lush green lawn. It must have cost a fortune, Tenny thought, to maintain in this climate and soil. The bay, lawn and dune all met on the south side of the house. The only access was by the north road. A car or even a person coming down the barren road would be visible long before drawing near to the house. The Sousas could not have picked a better fort.

He had been crouched on the sand dune for almost twenty-four hours and still the opportunity had not presented itself. The ankle which he had broken in his fall was throbbing and continued to swell, although it was tightly wrapped and splinted. He took some more Advil and thought that he was lucky he'd only cracked one bone on those damn stairs.

He swore aloud. What had started as a simple surveillance job was becoming more and more complicated with each passing hour. He'd been told to just watch the family and make sure nothing unusual happened. He'd been told about the woman police officer and given specific instructions in case she happened to show up in Brazil. It should've been easy money.

Then the family had slipped out of Ouro Preto right under his nose. The next day, before he could figure out his next move, the policewoman had arrived. Suddenly, his job was no longer to watch — it was to eliminate any chance of that little girl making it home. Cursing himself, he knew he'd made a mistake by not just leaving Ouro Preto and coming here to finish the job immediately. He thought it would be easier to eliminate strangers in this eccentric country. It would not have been a big deal, not as big as killing the Sousas. Now he had no choice. That bitch had escaped the other night and again she was too close. He knew that he needed to get to the family before she did.

He held up the blackened binoculars to get another look at the bitch. It was pretty fucking stupid of her to be sitting out in the open like that, as if he didn't even exist. If he had a more powerful rifle he could have ended it right now. He held his position on the dune behind the house. From this spot he could cover the road, the rear and the front of the house. He knew that they were home. They would come out soon and then it would be over. In the meantime, if that cop got too close he would take care of her.

He lowered the binoculars and shifted his weight again, quietly cursing at his inability to move and stretch. Waiting was not his strength. If he was at home where he knew how things worked he would just bust in and shoot them up. But this wasn't home and he was too far from an airport to risk it. The heavily tinted windows prevented him from being able to sight in on his targets, taking away his last option. Waiting was all he had left. It was worth his discomfort. With the money he was making from this job, he wouldn't ever have to do this stuff again. He glanced at his watch and as he did so the setting sun bounced penetrating rays off its face.

"Shit." He ducked down as if it would make a difference.

"Come on, let's get out of here." Tenny stood up quickly.

"Hey, what's the hurry?" Jorge protested as Tenny grabbed him by the wrist and dragged him to his feet. "Hey, that hurts."

"Get in the goddamn car." Tenny yanked open the passenger door and threw him in. "He's here. Shit, he's been watching us." Tenny rushed around to the front of the car and slammed the hood back into place. The reflection at first had only been a small irritant to her already tired eyes, but its true significance had followed quickly behind the flash of light.

Tenny got in, started the car and spun it around, heading back to Salvador. She had no idea how she was going to reach Kelsey, but she knew it would have to be soon. He was there, waiting, and there was no way to warn her.

Chapter Twenty-eight

"*Como via?*" Jorge greeted the waiter as they entered the small restaurant. The waiter welcomed them and eyed Jorge suspiciously as he led them to a table on the balcony overlooking the bay.

Jorge didn't miss a beat. "I run errands for the owner here in exchange for leftovers. It is a good place and always quiet. A good place to come and plan our mission."

Tenny was ignoring the boy. Carter sat down next to him and kissed the top of his head. "You have already done so much. I think we can handle it from here."

Jorge pulled away. "I'm not a child. This is a business arrangement. Ms. Tenacity hired me to help and my employment is not over until your daughter is safe." He

215

redirected his attention to Tenny. "I'm an honorable man and I have given my word."

Tenny finally spoke without looking at Jorge. Her tone was cold, she knew, her words chosen carefully. "You are not a man. You are still a boy with many things left to learn about life."

Jorge said nothing as he focused on Tenny. She watched him, waiting for the angry outburst of a hurt child. What she saw was the peace settle over him. He sat quietly, his gaze down. His shoulders relaxed and his hands fell from the table to his lap. His body became so calm that she could no longer see him breathing. At last he spoke and even his voice had lost the urgency of a child trying to be heard.

"My mother told me that every day of the rest of my life would be spent learning and teaching. She said that when a person stops doing this, the soul ceases to exist. A person without a soul is only another animal and will eventually begin to behave as the animals do." He leaned into the table, cocked his eyebrow and lowered his voice. "So, Ms. Tenacity, tell me, do you have all the answers?"

Tenny allowed herself to look at him. His eyes showed the blackness of a coal ready to be lit. "No, but I do know the most important answer of them all."

It was as if Jorge knew what she was about to say. He began to shake his head in disbelief. "And what one is that?"

She purposely spoke as if to a three-year-old. "That for some questions, problems and mysteries, there are no answers."

"That is your fear speaking, not your soul." Jorge leaned back from the table but would not release Tenny's gaze. "I have no fear. I will find all the answers."

Tenny was curious. "What answers do you seek?"

"That is easy. Here, in my country, we have many laws, but no rules. We are a great country that is being held back, not by a lack of spirit among the people. Instead it is the greed of a few that prevents us from bringing true equality to our people." Jorge smiled. "Therefore, I must find the answer of how to stop the greed."

"You are a foolish boy." Tenny laughed at him.

Then for an instant, the child emerged. He snapped, "I'm not!" Jorge stubbornly crossed his arms. Tenny did the same. They stared at each other.

Carter broke the silence. "You two only think you're on opposite ends of a journey."

They both looked at her. Jorge said, "I like you. You are the mystic, like my mother was. You spend your life not in search of answers, but instead in search of life itself. It's not the thoughts, but the feelings. It's not the ideas, but the actions." He turned back to Tenny. "Every great leader must have a mystic by their side."

Tenny laughed and finally conceded.

Carter was driving so that Tenny could think as they rolled along the beachfront drive. Jorge sat quietly in the back seat.

Suddenly they found their car trapped between two farming trucks loaded with young men and women laughing and dancing in the beds. As they moved forward, the pace on the road slowed as it became crowded with cars and more trucks carrying even more youth. After a few moments, Tenny began to feel the pound of the bass in her chest.

She rolled her window down and the blast of the music swept through the car. "What's going on?"

Jorge leaned forward. "Ah, I almost forgot. It is festival." The music grew louder and soon the youth began to abandon the trucks held in place by congestion. Jorge warned, "It's close, here we must turn before it is too late."

Carter forced the car over a portion of the sidewalk and down a side street. But before they were around the corner, they all caught a glimpse of what approached. Thousands and thousands of people surrounding a tractor-trailer rig that hosted nothing but speakers and amplifiers. The music was nearly deafening as it spread hundreds of yards into the night. The people — dancing, running, laughing, singing — advanced toward them. The crowd consuming everything in its path. Nothing was spared from its wild and dangerous joy.

"Here, stop the car," Jorge commanded. "I will meet you in the morning. The next left will lead you back to your hotel." They watched as he ran back into the crowd.

Carter drove to the next street and made a quick left turn.

"Shit! Look out!" Tenny shouted as she raised her hands to her eyes. She couldn't watch.

Carter laughed as she accelerated through the blaring horns of cars that didn't slow at the threat. "That little shit sent us down a one-way street." Carter swerved through traffic to the next intersection where she turned out of the excitement.

"It's okay now, Ms. Tenacity." Carter couldn't stop laughing. Jorge had the last word — the Brazilian way.

Chapter Twenty-nine

He wearily raised the binoculars to his half-closed eyes. His fatigue was severe, causing him to be unsure whether the boy was actually there across the bay, or just a mirage. The assassin watched as the boy from yesterday worked his way down to the edge of the water and prepared to begin a morning of fishing.

The boy had arrived with the sun, which was crawling upward in the sky. Today the sun's heat had arrived well before dawn and already the warmth had become unbearable. The camouflage clothing that the assassin wore was melting him into the side of the dune. If the family did not come out of the house soon, he would have no other choice but to go in and end this hunt. Especially now. The boy meant that the cop woman was also around somewhere and she was preparing to make her move.

He swept the area with the binoculars, looking for a waiting car or the woman. The road was barren. The only movements were the waves of heat rippling the static surroundings. The binoculars moved up the road toward the house as he completed what he considered to be a wasteful precaution. Nobody was going to make a move in or out of that house. He brought the binoculars down and touched the weapon which lay in his lap. It would all end soon.

It was difficult for her to see from their cramped hiding place, and her thoughts continuously drifted as she scanned the area.

The movement on the other side of the bay captured her attention. Ashley focused on a small boy who had appeared on the other side of the bay. She nudged Steve and gestured toward the boy. They did not speak, not wanting to risk even a whisper in the still silence. Steve took a quick look at the boy with the binoculars, then focused back on the house.

Ashley was frustrated by her inability to assist. Steve blocked her view of the house and the road. There was nothing important for her to watch, so to prevent boredom, Ashley watched the boy as he unpacked his fishing rod, a blanket and some bait. He settled down and began to cast his line into the mirrored water. Ashley watched the agitated water ringlets travel out from the disturbance and then disappear. She wondered when the first fish would bite.

* * * * *

220

"Okay, there he is. We're in a perfect place." Carter didn't lower the binoculars as she spoke.

Tenny responded weakly as she closed her eyes and tried to force the floating sensation from her head. The water was calm, but even the gentle rocking was causing her vision to spin. The sweat dripping from her forehead had nothing to do with the heat. Her hands shook not from adrenaline. The heaviness of her legs would not be relieved by stretching. Tenny was sure that if she unclenched her jaw, she would lose what little she had left in her stomach. The ride from the dock to the mouth of the bay had left her feeling extremely ill. All she could think about was getting off this damn boat which Jorge had procured.

Carter spoke again without looking away from the boy. "This is going to work, babe. It's the perfect plan. All we have to do is wait for his signal." She hesitated. "A child saving another child. I wonder if there's some type of meaning to how this has worked out." Carter didn't pause for Tenny to respond, which was good because Tenny couldn't open her mouth. "I mean, during this whole drama it's been the adults that have been the cause, the ones committing the crime, the ones trying to salvage a family. But when it comes right down to it, Kelsey's savior will be a child. There's got to be a reason why we are so dependent on Jorge."

Carter became silent again, but never took the binoculars off of Jorge. Tenny knew that she was right, but was stunned by the thought. Then Angelica's face came to Tenny. The rescue had started with the courage of a child grown beyond her years, searching her mind for the face of violence. Tenny took a deep breath, trying to control herself. They would save Kelsey — if Tenny could keep herself together long enough.

"That's it!"

Jorge lay back as if enjoying the heat of the day. It was the signal. The Sousas were on the move.

Carter threw the binoculars to the floor and slammed her finger into the ignition button. The engine roared as Carter yanked back on the throttle. The boat felt as if it actually raised up off the water as it jumped forward, tumbling Tenny to the floor. Carter spun the boat into the narrow mouth of the bay.

The house suddenly came into view and there, less than one hundred yards from her, was Kelsey.

Carter cranked on the wheel and forced the boat into a tighter turn, releasing a huge spray of water as the boat slid across the sleek surface. Kelsey looked up at the commotion. The rocks she had been gathering in her hands dropped to the ground.

"Steer away! Steer north!" Tenny was kneeling by Carter, clutching the wheel, moving them away from Kelsey. In the excitement, Carter had clearly forgotten the plan, forgotten the danger.

She started to scream above the roar of the engine. "Run, baby, run!" Frantically she waved at Kelsey as Tenny succeeded in veering the boat north. "Kelsey, baby, run! This way! Please, baby, run!"

They were only thirty yards from the shore. Kelsey was leaping and running, laughing then crying as she followed the water to the north end of the property. They were so close they could see her lips moving. Kelsey was yelling for her mommy.

He snapped the weapon up from his lap, but arranging it against his shoulder proved difficult with his movement-starved, numb limbs. The child rushed down to the water as the Sousas went around toward the garage.

He would be able to eliminate all three in moments. As he sighted in on the child, he smiled.

Suddenly a speedboat blasted around the entrance to the bay. At the unexpected noise he lifted his head from the weapon. He instantly knew who it was speeding toward the house from bay.

"Shit, shit! Why didn't I think of that? It's so fucking obvious!" He rushed to regain the child in his weapon's sights.

She was running toward the north end of the house. The woman driving the boat was frantically waving as she directed the boat toward the shore. Yet she was steering to the extreme north end of the property, the only corner where his shot would be blocked by the house. They were purposefully drawing the child out of his range. Desperately he sought to get the child in his sights before she disappeared. He caught her for a moment. Steadily he squeezed the trigger.

"What the hell is going on?" Ashley spun around. A speedboat was rushing into the bay, too fast, nearly out of control. A child was running in front of the white house at the end of the bay. Instantly she realized their mistake.

"We had the wrong house. There they are!" Ashley lunged down the side of the dune with Steve right behind her.

Everything was happening so fast, Ashley didn't have time to comprehend the situation. She couldn't concentrate. Then, above all the other noise, she heard the unmistakable sound of a rifle shot. She looked back at the dune. There, within striking distance of a 9mm, was a man bringing his rifle down and jumping to his feet. If she'd been armed, she would have dropped the asshole that second.

The man leaped through the sand and brush toward the house. Ashley didn't know who had been his target and she didn't want to look. The branches of the bushes jabbed and cut her skin as she recklessly pursued him. The memory of the airport hallway flashed through her mind. That time, she had allowed a killer to escape. This time she would not. She careened down the side of the dune.

The shaking in her hands had spread to her arms. She had lost her strength. Her legs, equally useless, began to cramp. Nauseous, Tenny realized that they were still speeding toward the beach which was perilously close. The scene blurred. All she knew was what she heard. The engine roared — still too loud. Carter screamed a warning — the panic in her voice escalating. Then the crack of the shot — a shot from a rifle. Tenny forced herself to focus. Somebody was about to die.

The first thing she saw was Sousa's chest explode with a flash of red. Then the ground inches from Kelsey was torn up as a bullet burrowed into the softness. Kelsey froze as Sousa collapsed to the ground a short distance behind her.

Tenny forced herself to her feet. "No! No! Don't stop! Kelsey, keep running, please, baby, keep running."

Next, Tenny witnessed a strength and a love that she would never see again. Carlota Sousa didn't even slow to weep for her fallen husband. Never breaking stride, she swept Kelsey into her arms and ran full force toward the north end of the beach.

Carter was still yelling, but Tenny suddenly realized there was another strange noise. "Oh shit!" It was the engine; it was still too loud. Carter was so concerned about

Kelsey that she hadn't slowed the rocketing speed of the craft.

"Pull back! Pull back!" Tenny screamed as she grabbed the throttle and yanked it back. At the same moment Carter gasped and spun the wheel hard to left, sending the boat into a broadside slide.

The impact with the shore crushed the side of the boat and sent Tenny flying. She had no doubt what the end would bring. Thudding to the ground, she was thankful for the soft, loose sand and weedy grass. Still the impact battered her already tender body, and once again the weapon which she had tucked into her pants smashed into her hip. She was thankful for the pain. As long as she hurt, she was conscious, alive and able to fight back.

Grabbing at her semi-automatic, she watched as Carlota and Kelsey leaped into the wreckage of the boat. Relief grabbed at her heart as she saw Carter rise and catch her daughter mid-air as Carlota passed her off. They were gone from sight as Carter dove for the protection of the boat's mangled frame.

Tenny crouched but could not stand. The spinning in her head was worse, and for a moment the darkness started to creep from the edges of her vision. She pleaded to whatever force might be listening, "No! Please, not now. Let me finish this." The darkness was pushed back and Tenny struggled to her feet.

Starting toward the boat, Tenny felt like she was walking through one of those spinning tunnels they always had at amusement parks when she was growing up. The ground beneath her felt like it was moving from under her feet. Each step forward was accompanied by a lurch to the side to steady her. At the end of the tunnel was the boat, but with each step it seemed to get farther away. She didn't have much time. He was still out there.

Chapter Thirty

The pain in his ankle was dulled by anger. He knew that his simple job had become impossibly complex due to that bitch and his own lack of anticipation. But enough was enough — it was going to end.

As he tumbled through the heavier brush near the driveway, the rifle strap snagged on a thick branch. He abandoned it in his rush to finish the job, and as he limped and hopped across the driveway, he drew his semi-automatic handgun. It was all he would need.

He rounded the corner of the house and started to cross the large lawn. Before him, the lifeless body of Sousa lay about halfway between him and the crashed boat. Nobody else was in sight except for the bitch, who seemed unaware of his presence. He knew the others had to be hidden in the boat — there was nowhere else to go.

A weapon hung helplessly at her side as she limped toward the boat. She was hurt. He smiled as he brought up his own weapon to put her out of her misery. She was not his equal. The pain had caused her to become careless, while he had channeled his own pain into strength. As he squeezed the trigger he thought, women make horrible killers.

Tenny dove to the ground. She felt the heat enter her right shoulder. The burning path left her arm and tore into her side just below her breast. The bullet met bone as it crashed into her rib. There was an explosion of pain as the bone shattered. Tenny couldn't breathe, but she could hear herself gasping for air. She couldn't feel her right arm, but she could sense the gush of blood from her wounds. She couldn't think, but her mind was automatically transmitting the desperate plea of an officer down and in need of assistance.

Every cop knows they have a chance of being shot. They all accept that risk. They also all know that if it's ever them, they won't go down alone. In her heart Tenny was a cop — she was going to end this. She rolled over her paralyzed right side, toward the gun which had been torn from her grip by the power of the shot. She seized the weapon and Tenny's world began to move in slow motion. Her vision crystallized. Her thoughts became precise.

The assassin was only a few feet from the boat. Tenny watched. She could see his finger pulling back on the trigger. It was too late. She fired.

The bullet from her unsteady gun traveled a direct path but only grazed him. He flinched and fired carelessly into the front of the boat. Then Tenny prepared to die.

She let her weapon drop in front of her. The assassin approached her. Tenny thought, *Come on bastard, come on in closer. I won't miss this time. We're going together.*

There was no doubt in her mind that by the time he was close enough for her to snatch her gun and finish this, he'd be able to get off a shot. At the close range they would both die. Tenny simply prayed she'd be able to endure the pain long enough to return fire.

He was standing only a few feet away now — it was time. As Tenny lunged, something she didn't identify flashed in her peripheral vision. A shot popped, but there was no pain. There was nothing. Then a body dropped on her.

"Shit! I'm sorry." Ashley rolled off Tenny and started to scramble on all fours across the ground. She had not seen Tenny's weapon lying next to them and was trying to reach the assassin's before he gathered himself up.

Tenny watched as he picked himself off the ground and then threw himself back at it to retrieve her weapon. Ashley had gotten there first. But he had Tenny's gun. The two of them were locked in a deadly stand-off, weapons pointed at each other, waiting for the other to make the move.

The last shot came from the assassin's own rifle. Steve had retrieved it as it dangled in the brush. He had only been waiting for a clear shot.

Chapter Thirty-one

"So, Your Honor, will you issue the arrest warrants?"
Caroline's only response was silence. Tenny knew that he
would. How could he do anything else after listening to the
depositions provided by Carlota Sousa and Kelsey?

Finally the judge said, "I expect you down here within
the hour, Skates, to pick up two no-bail arrest warrants. I
also expect them to be in custody within minutes of those
warrants being received. In addition, I expect you to have
a list on my desk by morning of any and all FBI personnel
involved in child-abduction investigations over the last ten
years." He paused. "Now, Officer Mendoza, if you'll excuse
me I need to call the Attorney General. I'm sure she

would like to hear all this. I'm looking forward to meeting you."

"Thank you, Your Honor, and when you do, it's just Tenny."

"Well, we'll see about that. Good night. See you in an hour, Skates."

"Yes, Your Honor." Caroline waited until she was sure the third line had disconnected. "You're still there, aren't you?"

"I'm here."

The professional tone left Caroline's voice, replaced entirely by concern. "Are you okay?"

Tenny laughed weakly. "I'm coming home, aren't I?"

Caroline sighed. "I'm glad it's all over for you."

"Well, you have Carlota Sousa to thank for that. She could have said anything, had us all thrown into prison, but she told the truth." Tenny took a deep breath, she was so tired. "Without Carlota we wouldn't have made it out of Brazil and we wouldn't have enough to stop the Jenkinses. Without your help, we never would have found Kelsey."

"Spoken like a true leader," Caroline said softly.

"Yeah, that's me." Tenny replaced the phone into the back of the seat ahead of her. She made a quick visual check around the plane. Ashley and Steve were sleeping across the aisle. Tenny guessed that they probably hadn't slept in days. Once again, the sight of her friends, her partners, gave her a sense of relief. Knowing that two people would always be there to support her no matter what gave Tenny a feeling of security that she had really never experienced before. She was lucky.

Carlota was stretched out on the seats in the row just in front of Steve and Ashley. Tenny suspected that Carlota would be haunted for a long time.

Carter rested her head on Tenny's good shoulder. She wasn't sleeping but watching her slumbering daughter, whom Carter clutched to her chest. They hadn't released each other from the moment Kelsey found her way back to her mother's arms.

Tenny glanced outside the window at the early morning sky. The airplane had moved to a higher elevation and was flying over a storm. Below Tenny were dark, fast-moving clouds. Which was moving with greater speed, she wondered, the storm or the plane? Suddenly there was a crack of lightning.

From above the lightning did not strike, it ignited. The clouds flashed red, reflected by the rising sun. The redness filled the sky and then was gone. The clouds rolled over and then again filled with light. She had never seen anything like it. Everything appeared much different from above.

Carter said, "How's that shoulder?" She obviously had something else on her mind, but didn't seem to know how to start.

"I don't know what Sousas' doctor gave me, but I'm not feeling any pain."

Carter touched Tenny's face. "Good." Then there was another long pause as she simply stared at Tenny. Finally she asked, "What will happen when we get back?"

"Everything's going to be fine. By the time we land, the Jenkinses will be in custody, and they won't ever get out."

Carter looked like she'd been struck by another bullet. "I didn't mean that. I meant, what will happen to you? What will happen to us?"

Tenny reached out and touched her face as a tear fell from Carter's eye. "Babe, I don't know what's going to happen." Tenny wiped away the second tear. "You're the mystic woman, you tell me."

A few of the publications of
THE NAIAD PRESS, INC.
P.O. Box 10543 • Tallahassee, Florida 32302
Phone (904) 539-5965
Toll-Free Order Number: 1-800-533-1973
Mail orders welcome. Please include 15% postage.
Write or call for our free catalog which also features an
incredible selection of lesbian videos.

THE SEARCH by Melanie McAllester. 240 pp. Exciting top cop
Tenny Mendoza case. ISBN 1-56280-150-3 $10.95

THE WISH LIST by Saxon Bennett. 192 pp. Romance through
the years. ISBN 1-56280-125-2 10.95

FIRST IMPRESSIONS by Kate Calloway. 208 pp. P.I. Cassidy
James' first case. ISBN 1-56280-133-3 10.95

OUT OF THE NIGHT by Kris Bruyer. 192 pp. Spine-tingling
thriller. ISBN 1-56280-120-1 10.95

NORTHERN BLUE by Tracey Richardson. 224 pp. Police recruits
Miki & Miranda — passion in the line of fire. ISBN 1-56280-118-X 10.95

LOVE'S HARVEST by Peggy Herring. 176 pp. by the author of
Once More With Feeling. ISBN 1-56280-117-1 10.95

THE COLOR OF WINTER by Lisa Shapiro. 208 pp. Romantic
love beyond your wildest dreams. ISBN 1-56280-116-3 10.95

FAMILY SECRETS by Laura DeHart Young. 208 pp. Enthralling
romance and suspense. ISBN 1-56280-119-8 10.95

INLAND PASSAGE by Jane Rule. 288 pp. Tales exploring conven-
tional & unconventional relationships. ISBN 0-930044-56-8 10.95

DOUBLE BLUFF by Claire McNab. 208 pp. 7th Detective Carol
Ashton Mystery. ISBN 1-56280-096-5 10.95

BAR GIRLS by Lauran Hoffman. 176 pp. See the movie, read
the book! ISBN 1-56280-115-5 10.95

THE FIRST TIME EVER edited by Barbara Grier & Christine
Cassidy. 272 pp. Love stories by Naiad Press authors.
ISBN 1-56280-086-8 14.95

MISS PETTIBONE AND MISS McGRAW by Brenda Weathers.
208 pp. A charming ghostly love story. ISBN 1-56280-151-1 10.95

CHANGES by Jackie Calhoun. 208 pp. Involved romance and
relationships. ISBN 1-56280-083-3 10.95

FAIR PLAY by Rose Beecham. 256 pp. 3rd Amanda Valentine
Mystery.   ISBN 1-56280-081-7   10.95

PAXTON COURT by Diane Salvatore. 256 pp. Erotic and wickedly
funny contemporary tale about the business of learning to live
together.   ISBN 1-56280-109-0   21.95

PAYBACK by Celia Cohen. 176 pp. A gripping thriller of romance,
revenge and betrayal.   ISBN 1-56280-084-1   10.95

THE BEACH AFFAIR by Barbara Johnson. 224 pp. Sizzling
summer romance/mystery/intrigue.   ISBN 1-56280-090-6   10.95

GETTING THERE by Robbi Sommers. 192 pp. Nobody does it
like Robbi!   ISBN 1-56280-099-X   10.95

FINAL CUT by Lisa Haddock. 208 pp. 2nd Carmen Ramirez
Mystery.   ISBN 1-56280-088-4   10.95

FLASHPOINT by Katherine V. Forrest. 256 pp. A Lesbian
blockbuster!   ISBN 1-56280-079-5   10.95

CLAIRE OF THE MOON by Nicole Conn. Audio Book —Read
by Marianne Hyatt.   ISBN 1-56280-113-9   16.95

FOR LOVE AND FOR LIFE: INTIMATE PORTRAITS OF
LESBIAN COUPLES by Susan Johnson. 224 pp.
                                            ISBN 1-56280-091-4   14.95

DEVOTION by Mindy Kaplan. 192 pp. See the movie — read
the book!   ISBN 1-56280-093-0   10.95

SOMEONE TO WATCH by Jaye Maiman. 272 pp. 4th Robin
Miller Mystery.   ISBN 1-56280-095-7   10.95

GREENER THAN GRASS by Jennifer Fulton. 208 pp. A young
woman — a stranger in her bed.   ISBN 1-56280-092-2   10.95

TRAVELS WITH DIANA HUNTER by Regine Sands. Erotic
lesbian romp. Audio Book (2 cassettes)   ISBN 1-56280-107-4   16.95

CABIN FEVER by Carol Schmidt. 256 pp. Sizzling suspense
and passion.   ISBN 1-56280-089-1   10.95

THERE WILL BE NO GOODBYES by Laura DeHart Young. 192
pp. Romantic love, strength, and friendship.   ISBN 1-56280-103-1   10.95

FAULTLINE by Sheila Ortiz Taylor. 144 pp. Joyous comic
lesbian novel.   ISBN 1-56280-108-2   9.95

OPEN HOUSE by Pat Welch. 176 pp. 4th Helen Black Mystery.
                                            ISBN 1-56280-102-3   10.95

ONCE MORE WITH FEELING by Peggy J. Herring. 240 pp.
Lighthearted, loving romantic adventure.   ISBN 1-56280-089-2   10.95

FOREVER by Evelyn Kennedy. 224 pp. Passionate romance — love
overcoming all obstacles.   ISBN 1-56280-094-9   10.95

WHISPERS by Kris Bruyer. 176 pp. Romantic ghost story
                                            ISBN 1-56280-082-5   10.95

NIGHT SONGS by Penny Mickelbury. 224 pp. 2nd Gianna Maglione
Mystery.   ISBN 1-56280-097-3   10.95

GETTING TO THE POINT by Teresa Stores. 256 pp. Classic
southern Lesbian novel.   ISBN 1-56280-100-7   10.95

PAINTED MOON by Karin Kallmaker. 224 pp. Delicious
Kallmaker romance.   ISBN 1-56280-075-2   10.95

THE MYSTERIOUS NAIAD edited by Katherine V. Forrest &
Barbara Grier. 320 pp. Love stories by Naiad Press authors.
                                            ISBN 1-56280-074-4   14.95

DAUGHTERS OF A CORAL DAWN by Katherine V. Forrest.
240 pp. Tenth Anniversay Edition.   ISBN 1-56280-104-X   10.95

BODY GUARD by Claire McNab. 208 pp. 6th Carol Ashton
Mystery.   ISBN 1-56280-073-6   10.95

CACTUS LOVE by Lee Lynch. 192 pp. Stories by the beloved
storyteller.   ISBN 1-56280-071-X   9.95

SECOND GUESS by Rose Beecham. 216 pp. 2nd Amanda Valentine
Mystery.   ISBN 1-56280-069-8   9.95

THE SURE THING by Melissa Hartman. 208 pp. L.A. earthquake
romance.   ISBN 1-56280-078-7   9.95

A RAGE OF MAIDENS by Lauren Wright Douglas. 240 pp. 6th Caitlin
Reece Mystery.   ISBN 1-56280-068-X   10.95

TRIPLE EXPOSURE by Jackie Calhoun. 224 pp. Romantic drama
involving many characters.   ISBN 1-56280-067-1   9.95

UP, UP AND AWAY by Catherine Ennis. 192 pp. Delightful
romance.   ISBN 1-56280-065-5   9.95

PERSONAL ADS by Robbi Sommers. 176 pp. Sizzling short
stories.   ISBN 1-56280-059-0   9.95

FLASHPOINT by Katherine V. Forrest. 256 pp. Lesbian
blockbuster!   ISBN 1-56280-043-4   22.95

CROSSWORDS by Penny Sumner. 256 pp. 2nd Victoria Cross
Mystery.   ISBN 1-56280-064-7   9.95

SWEET CHERRY WINE by Carol Schmidt. 224 pp. A novel of
suspense.   ISBN 1-56280-063-9   9.95

CERTAIN SMILES by Dorothy Tell. 160 pp. Erotic short stories.
                                            ISBN 1-56280-066-3   9.95

These are just a few of the many Naiad Press titles — we are the oldest and
largest lesbian/feminist publishing company in the world. Please request a
complete catalog. We offer personal service; we encourage and welcome
direct mail orders from individuals who have limited access to bookstores
carrying our publications.